DEVINE'S LAW

In his twenty-five years of law enforcement, Marshal Jake T. Devine has always brought in his man with a bullet blasted between the eyes. So when Max Randall shoots his mouth off, claiming he knows a devastating secret about wealthy rancher Roy Cowie, he's spoiling for trouble. Cowie calls in Devine and, without provocation, the brutal marshal slaughters Max's entire family. Max heads for the hills with Devine and his deadly Peacemaker in hot pursuit. Can Max survive long enough to reveal what he knows?

Books by I. J. Parnham
in the Linford Western Library:

THE OUTLAWED DEPUTY
THE LAST RIDER FROM HELL
BAD DAY IN DIRTWOOD

I. J. PARNHAM

DEVINE'S LAW

Complete and Unabridged

LINFORD
Leicester

First published in Great Britain in 2004 by
Robert Hale Limited
London

First Linford Edition
published 2005
by arrangement with
Robert Hale Limited
London

The moral right of the author
has been asserted

British Library CIP Data

Parnham, I. J.
 Devine's law.—Large print ed.—
 Linford western library
 1. Western stories
 2. Large type books
 I. Title
 823.9'2 [F]

 ISBN 1–84395–614–4

Published by
F. A. Thorpe (Publishing)
Anstey, Leicestershire

Set by Words & Graphics Ltd.
Anstey, Leicestershire
Printed and bound in Great Britain by
T. J. International Ltd., Padstow, Cornwall

This book is printed on acid-free paper

1

Marshal Jake T. Devine kicked open the door of the shack to crash it back against the wall.

Inside, Seth Randall and his three rough-clad youngsters sat at a table.

'Howdy,' Jake muttered, his vast frame filling the doorway.

'What you want?' Seth snarled.

'Max.'

'Then you've wasted a journey.' Seth rocked his chair back and folded his arms. 'He ain't here.'

Jake took a long pace forward and glanced around the shack. Aside from the table and chairs it was bare of furniture. Propped against the back wall were a row of rifles. Two ripening buck carcasses hung from the ceiling, swaying in the breeze from the open door.

'I'm guessing you're Seth Randall

and these are your sons. How do I know one of them ain't Max?'

The eldest of Seth's boys pushed from his chair and strode two paces to stand on Jake's right side. Another boy stood to Jake's left.

'That's Adam and Wayne,' Seth said. 'Caleb's sitting by me. As I said — Max ain't here. So scat.'

Jake smiled. 'You only have four sons?'

Seth matched the smile. 'Yup. Four sons are more than enough for any man to keep.'

Jake glanced at Adam and chuckled. 'Guessing he's the runt of your litter. Hard to believe anyone could produce someone uglier than him.'

'Why you . . . ' Adam shouted. He whirled round, flailing his fist in a round-arm punch.

With his forearm Jake deflected the punch and kicked Adam's shin, tumbling him to the floor. He twitched his hand, pulling his Peacemaker. 'You people ain't being co-operative, but that'll change.' With his other hand Jake grabbed Wayne's collar. He dragged him close and slammed the gun barrel between his eyes. 'Where's your brother?'

As Wayne gulped, Seth held his arms wide.

'We don't want trouble,' he babbled. 'None of us are packing guns.'

'You have rifles.'

Seth pushed his chair back and stood.

'We only use them to hunt. We're no threat to you.' He sighed. 'And I don't know where Max is. He took off late last night.'

'Where to?' Jake asked, rolling the words.

'Don't know. Time's long past when Max told me what he was doing.'

Jake tightened his grip, hoisting Wayne on to his tiptoes. He glared deep into Wayne's eyes.

'What's Max done?' Wayne said between gasps.

Jake pressed the gun tight against Wayne's forehead, the skin buckling around the barrel.

'*That* is an interesting question. It says you might tell me where he is, but it depends what he's done.' Jake pressed the gun harder, forcing Wayne to lean back so that his head and shoulders were parallel to the floor. 'Talk to me or your pa will have one less son to feed this winter.'

'You wouldn't,' Wayne whispered.

'Wrong answer.'

Jake twitched his finger, the gunshot echoing in the shack. As Wayne collapsed from his grip, he swung the gun round, shooting Adam and Caleb through the stomach and chest. He whirled the gun back to Seth.

In open-mouthed shock, Seth collapsed to his knees. He held out a shaking hand, pointing beside Jake.

'Adam,' he murmured.

Jake glanced to his side. On the dusty floor Adam still writhed, holding his stomach. With a contemptuous flick of the wrist, Jake fired and Adam collapsed, his last breath rustling a flurry of dust.

4

'You'll pay for what you've . . . '
Seth's voice faded to a croaked whisper.

'Tough talking for an unarmed man facing my gun,' Jake roared, holding his Peacemaker at arm's length. 'Now where's Max?'

Seth snarled his top lip. 'You don't think I'm answering, do you?'

'Nope.'

Jake fired twice more. He sauntered three paces to stand over Seth's body and spat on his bloodied forehead.

He reloaded and cocked his head to one side, listening. Silence had descended on the shack, punctuated by the breeze whistling around the door. When he'd confirmed that no surprises would come, he kicked open the other two doors in the shack.

Both rooms were empty, but in the second room the shutters were open. Jake stood, confirming the room was as cold as the wind blowing in from outside — so the window had been open a while.

With his Peacemaker raised to his

shoulder, Jake edged to the window and glanced through. Nobody was outside. Still, Jake slipped through the window and sidled around the side of the shack.

In the corral at the back two horses bustled against the rough fence, the same number as when he'd arrived.

Jake checked the hoof-prints around the corral. Dust filled them. With his hand to his brow, he surveyed the surrounding hills, searching for dust clouds on the horizon. As he saw none, Jake returned to the shack.

He gathered the rifles and laid one beside each body. Then he strode outside, leapt on his horse, and headed back to Carmon.

As Jake rode down the trail, he whistled.

* * *

The coach lurched to a stop ten miles from Carmon. Gabe stretched his aching back, then pushed open the door and stepped outside.

The driver, Randolph, had wandered into the trading post and, as this was the only building on the crossroads of the north-south and east-west trails, Gabe followed him.

The trading post was basic. Sawdust coated the floor. The drinking area lacked tables and chairs. For a bar, two planks were atop upturned barrels. Aside from Randolph, the only other customers were two scrawny cowhands who leaned against the back wall and three more smartly dressed men standing by the side wall. Each group guffawed and slapped each others' backs, sharing the incomprehensible humour of the over-drunk.

'Whiskey or beer?' Randolph asked when Gabe joined him.

'Beer.'

Randolph waved to the burly-armed bartender.

Burns coated the bartender's apron, suggesting that he was also a blacksmith. He wandered to a barrel by the wall and returned with two foaming and cloudy beers. He slammed them on the makeshift bar.

In a long swallow, Gabe drank half of his beer, then ran the back of his hand over his mouth, wiping away a moustache of froth.

At the back of the trading post, one of the scrawny cowhands slapped the other's shoulder.

'Anyhow, Max,' he shouted, 'what was you saying?'

'I was saying, Uncas,' Max slurred, thrusting out a leg as he fought to stay upright. 'Tor McFadden and Roy Cowie deserve everything that's coming to them. They ain't worth squat.'

Gabe turned and glared at Max, but Max faced the other men by the side wall. These men peeled away and strode to the centre of the room.

'You'll take that back,' Mort Falcon, the nearest man facing him, muttered. He lifted his fists, matched by Silas Fenshaw and Carl Perkins.

'Make me,' Max said, rolling his thin shoulders.

'Glad to oblige.'

In unison the three thickset men took a long pace towards the two smaller men.

Gabe slammed down his drink and sauntered from the bar.

'What in tarnation is this fight about?' he asked, staring at Mort.

'Don't know you, stranger,' Mort muttered, keeping his gaze on Max. 'But Max is mouthing off about Tor McFadden and Roy Cowie again. It's time to put an end to that.'

'And why does that concern you?'

'I'm one of Tor's ranch hands.'

Gabe chewed his bottom lip. 'And that's the only reason you'll beat him?'

'Do I need another?'

'Perhaps not, but three men against two ain't fair.' Gabe grinned. 'Three against three is fairer.'

With the back of his hand, Gabe hit Mort across the jaw for him to fly back and land on his side. Carrying his motion onward, Gabe ducked and charged at Carl. Leading with his shoulder he thundered into his chest and pushed him over a barrel. While Carl floundered on the floor, he kicked him hard in the stomach and spun round.

Silas's first blow had felled Uncas, but Max was squaring up.

He turned from Max's fight and stood between the two sprawling men. Mort stirred first. Gabe stormed two paces and punched him deep in the guts with a short arm-jab. As Mort folded, he kicked his chin for him to collapse in a heap. He dashed to Carl, who still clutched his stomach, and grabbed his collar. He dragged him across the floor and deposited him outside.

Gabe returned and smiled as Max dragged his vanquished assailant across the floor and matched Gabe's throw outside.

When Max returned, Gabe grabbed Mort's collar and stared at his bloodied face.

'If you don't want another beating,'

he muttered, 'stay out of my way.'

Before Mort retorted, Gabe pulled him to his feet and, with a nod shared with Max, they each grabbed an arm and threw Mort through the door.

Gabe patted his hands together and returned to the bar.

With an outstretched hand, Max dragged Uncas to his feet, then joined Gabe at the bar.

'I'm obliged.' Max patted Gabe's back. 'It's nice to have an ally. Ain't got many of those.'

'I ain't an ally,' Gabe said. 'I just hate to see bullies beating down on losers.'

'Either way, Uncas and me are much obliged.'

Gabe waved to the bartender and threw a coin on the bar.

'I'll have another drink. Got me a thirst.'

Max nudged his coin aside. 'Put your money away. I'll buy this.'

'No thanks.' Gabe shrugged his jacket closed. 'Ain't taking a drink from someone who insults Roy Cowie.'

While Max scratched his head, the bartender slammed the drink on the bar. Gabe took the brew and sauntered to the back wall. He sipped his drink while he flexed his shoulders.

'What's his problem?' Max asked Randolph.

Randolph chuckled. 'You should have asked him his name before you fought with him.'

'Who is he?'

'He's Gabe Cowie. Roy's son.'

'Roy Cowie's only got one son.' Max rubbed his sweating brow and turned to Uncas for confirmation.

'Yesterday he only had one,' Gabe whispered to himself, and hunched over his beer. 'Today he has two.'

2

When Gabe Cowie reached Carmon he jumped from the coach and glanced along the road. The sign he looked for was before him.

Once Randolph had thrown down his bag, Gabe hoisted it on his back and strode to the sheriff's office. He walked inside, but to his surprise the sheriff sitting behind the desk was a young man.

'What can I do for you?' the sheriff asked, glancing up.

'I've arrived on the coach. I'm looking for Sheriff Cowie.'

'You've found him.'

With drawing realization, Gabe nodded.

'Sheriff Roy Cowie,' he still said.

The sheriff leaned back in his chair. 'My pa hung up his star last year. He's our duly elected mayor now.'

Gabe sighed and edged from side to

side. 'Where is Roy now?'

'Pa will be back at the ranch.'

'In that case, I see no reason to delay this. You're Frank.'

'You have the advantage on me . . . ' The sheriff, Frank, cocked his head to one side. 'You ain't who I think you are, are you?'

Gabe couldn't stop a smile emerging. 'If you think I'm Gabe, you're right.'

With his face wreathed in a beaming smile, Frank rushed from behind his desk. He clamped Gabe's hand in a firm handshake and shook it with a solid lunge.

'I'm mighty pleased to have me a younger brother.'

Gabe squeezed Frank's hand. 'And I'm mighty pleased to have me an elder brother, Sheriff.'

Frank slipped his hand from Gabe's and perched on his desk with his arms folded. He tipped back his hat, still grinning.

'My brother can call me Frank.'

'Fine, Frank.' Gabe suppressed the

smile that was threatening to become a permanent feature. 'I didn't know if you'd know I was coming.'

'Your letter last year caused a whole mess of problems. Pa went quiet — not that we noticed at first. You know what he's like . . . ' Frank frowned. 'Perhaps you don't.'

'Nope.'

'Anyhow, we realized that something was wrong, but we waited. Eventually he called a family meeting and announced that . . . '

Frank stared from the window. When he looked back, Gabe thought he saw moisture in his eyes.

'Our ma died last fall,' Gabe said. 'I don't reckon she suffered much, not that she'd let on. You know what she was like.'

Frank matched Gabe's slight smile. 'Nope.'

'Anyhow, Ma never encouraged me to contact the rest of the family, but she didn't forbid me to either. So I wrote. I thought I ought to.'

15

'You did right.'

Gabe wandered across the office and sat on a spare desk. In shared understanding of the uncomfortable subject, they sat in silence, smiling at each other, until Gabe coughed.

'You were telling me about your meeting.'

'Yeah.' Frank shuffled back on the desk. 'Pa announced that our ma had died and that you'd asked if you could visit and heal the divisions. He said this was a family decision and that we had a vote on whether to encourage you.'

'Who voted for what?'

Frank frowned, then smiled. 'You're here, ain't you?'

'Suppose I am.'

'Can't have been easy for you to come.'

Gabe shrugged, rejecting several rehearsed speeches.

'It would have been harder not to come. I'm heading to New York to practise law. I could have found a route that avoided Carmon, but somehow

16

that didn't seem right.'

'That's a long journey. Ain't there enough bad guys in California?'

'I ain't that sort of lawyer.'

'Oh? What sort are you?'

As Gabe sighed, the door rattled open and crashed against the wall. A huge man filled the doorway. With his feet set wide he glared at Frank, his bushy beard bristling. The stale odour of unwashed clothes and caked-on sweat filled the room.

Gabe stood — ready to help Frank deal with this troublemaker.

'Any luck?' Frank asked.

'Nope,' the man said and strode into the office, dust cascading to the floor with every pace. 'Max wasn't there.'

'Would that be Max Randall?' Gabe asked.

The man glared at Gabe, narrowing his piercing blue eyes, his grime-filled wrinkles ridging.

'Who are you?' he grunted.

'This is my brother,' Frank said, 'Gabe Cowie. He's arrived from California.

And this is Marshal Jake T. Devine.'

The newcomer, Jake, nodded. 'You another lawman?'

'I'm a lawyer.'

Jake snorted. 'Ain't got time for lawyers. Where did you see Max?'

'He was in a trading post, ten miles west along the trail.'

Frank coughed. 'Told you that'd be a better place to try. Max ain't good for anything but drinking the trading post dry.'

Jake shrugged. 'Drinking with anyone in particular?'

Gabe rubbed his chin. 'Uncas Jackson.'

'Is Max still there?'

'He left before I did. That'd be about two hours ago. But Uncas was still there when I left.'

Frank rolled from his desk. 'Did Seth offer anything, Marshal?'

Jake rubbed fingers through his beard, chuckling. 'Nope.'

'Then I'll question him.'

'Seth won't tell you anything now.

Man turned a rifle on me. No one does that.'

'You killed him?' Frank whispered.

'Sure did.' Jake grinned with a wide arc of yellow teeth. 'He died along with the rest of his worthless family.'

Frank gulped and stared through his window.

'Seth Randall and three of his sons are dead.' Frank sounded as if he was talking to himself.

'Yeah. Max is the only one left. Pity he's the most worthless one.'

Frank turned to Jake. 'You can't do that.'

'When four men turn on you, you don't do anything but shoot to kill.'

While kneading his forehead, Frank stared at the floor.

'What's your plan?' he asked, his voice husky.

'I'll find Max. In two hours he won't have strayed far.' Jake strode to the door but stopped in the doorway. 'Don't suppose you'll tell me what Max has done before I fetch him.'

'No, but Jake . . . ' Frank slammed his fist on the desk, but Jake kept his back turned. 'When you bring Max in, bring him in alive.'

Without a backward glance, Jake strode into the road, leaving the door open.

Gabe turned to Frank. 'Why is that brute looking for Max?'

Frank slammed down his fist again. 'Pa called for him. Everyone knows about Marshal Jake Devine's methods, but Pa insisted.'

'A mayor can't tell a sheriff how to run his business.'

'Don't know for sure. Pa is Pa.'

'Guess having a former sheriff as your mayor can cause problems.' Gabe sighed. 'Although Devine seems a bigger problem.'

'Got no problem with his success rate, just his methods.'

'What did Max do?'

'It's a long story.'

'I have time for the short version.'

'To be honest I don't know all the

details.' Frank placed his hands on his hips. 'And I have to head out to Seth Randall's farm. I've some bodies to collect.'

Gabe stood to one side. 'I've taken enough of your time.'

'You ain't. I can swing by our ranch and leave you with Pa, or you can come with me and meet Pa later.'

Gabe frowned. 'Seth Randall's farm it is.'

* * *

Jake Devine stormed into the trading post. Inside, a mid-evening bustle filled the room.

Jake strode to the bar and slammed a fist on the wooden top, rattling nearby glasses.

The bartender wandered to him. 'Yeah, yeah, I'm serving as fast as I can.'

'I don't want a drink.' Jake leaned on the bar. It creaked beneath his elbows. 'I want Uncas Jackson.'

'Never heard of him.'

'You have.'

The bartender sneered, but as calls for beer came from further down the bar, he shrugged.

'He's in the poker-game.'

Jake tipped his hat and swirled round. He strode through the throng of people to the poker-game at the back of the room.

Four men sat on crates and hunched around a barrel. The pot on the barrel top contained a few nickels, the minuscule stakes not enticing anybody to watch the action.

Jake let his shadow fall over the nearest man, who looked up. Jake provided his best grin.

'Uncas Jackson.'

'He ain't here.' The man turned back to glare at his cards.

Jake turned as if to leave. Then with lightning speed, he grabbed the man's collar and dragged him from his crate. He thrust his gun deep into the man's back.

'That's a strange answer,' he muttered into the man's ear, 'because I reckon that *you* are Uncas Jackson.'

The man gulped and wriggled in Jake's grip.

'I ain't him,' he whined. He nodded at the scrawny man sitting opposite. 'He is.'

'Thank you kindly.' Jake threw the man back on to his crate and leaned on the barrel top. 'So, Uncas, why didn't you speak up?'

With his card hand shaking, Uncas shuffled back on his crate. 'I've done nothing to nobody and I don't know anything about anybody.'

Jake grinned. 'That's a mighty sweeping statement. But as Max Randall's friend I reckon you've done something to somebody at sometime.'

Uncas slumped on his crate. 'I ain't taking the blame for anything he's done. He's bad company.' Uncas glanced at the other card-players, who grunted their agreement. 'But I heard he took off. I guess you're the lawman who's looking for him.'

'You know plenty for a man who don't know anything about anybody.'

Jake grabbed the barrel rim and swung it to the side, knocking over the man sitting to his right. With a large hand he grabbed Uncas and pulled him to his feet, his cards showering around him.

'What you doing?' Uncas whined. 'I said I don't know where Max is.'

'I'm doing nothing. You're the one who's taking me on a journey.'

Jake tightened his grip and dragged Uncas across the floor. Uncas scrambled and kicked, trying to stand, but Jake built up a good pace.

At the doorway he threw Uncas outside and glanced back. The three other poker-players were righting the barrel and preparing to carry on their game. The other trading-post folk continued their conversations.

Outside, Uncas glared up and straightened his clothing.

'I don't know where Max is,' he said,

24

his voice shaking. 'Whatever you're planning won't change that.'

Jake hoisted Uncas to his feet and dragged him from the trading post.

'Which scrawny horse is yours?'

'That one.' Uncas pointed to a moth-eaten old bay. 'What do you want to know that for?'

'Get your scrawny hide on your scrawny horse and quit whining.' Jake threw Uncas to the ground.

With sudden defiance, Uncas rolled to his feet and set his hands on his hips.

'I can't take you anywhere,' he snapped.

Jake thrust his face to scant inches from Uncas's face.

'Then you and I will suffer each other's company for a long time, because you're staying with me until I find Max.' Jake bundled Uncas back and kicked his rump, hurrying him towards his bay. 'And if you ain't guessed it yet, I ain't relaxing company.'

Uncas gulped. 'I'll get on my horse.'

At Seth Randall's farm, Gabe jumped from the cart.

The low sun cast long shadows from the rotting wagons and collapsed fences, and the shack was the same style of half-sod homestead that Gabe was used to back home.

'All the Randall family lived here?' Gabe asked, kicking at a lump of metal. Too much rust coated the object for him to identify it.

'Yeah, they weren't neat. You can scout around outside if you want.'

'No, we'll check out the shack together.'

Frank opened his mouth, then closed it.

Gabe filed in behind Frank and strode into the building. In the oppressive heat flies buzzed around them.

As Jake had said, four bodies were inside. Three bodies lay on their backs before the door. The fourth lay across a

26

table. Beside each body a rifle lay.

Gabe closed his eyes a moment.

Frank ducked under a hanging carcass and knelt beside the nearest body, confirming what the flies already knew. He cranked open a rifle. It was loaded. Frank glanced up.

'You fine with this?'

Since Gabe had entered the shack he hadn't moved from the doorway. He coughed and strode inside. He knelt beside the first body, then flinched. The dead person was barely fifteen, his freckles and untamed hair hinting at the man he would never become.

'I never realized they'd be so young.'

Frank scratched his chin. 'Don't know their ages for sure, but Max is the eldest and he's about twenty.'

'What trouble can boys this age cause for Devine to kill them?'

'They got in the way of Marshal Jake T. Devine. Nobody does that.'

Gabe rubbed his forehead, judging whether Frank had spoken in admiration or disgust. He detected both.

A rifle lay beside the boy, but his hands were beneath his body.

'Devine said that they turned on him, but if that were so, wouldn't the body have the rifle in its hand?'

Frank tipped back his hat and scratched his forehead.

'Who can say? I've seen the aftermaths of gunfights and each situation is different. If Devine said they turned on him, that's what happened.'

'I guess few witnesses are left to confirm what happens whenever Devine investigates.'

'So I've heard.'

While Frank checked each body, Gabe wandered around the shack. As nothing of interest was in the main room, he examined the first side room. This contained a larder with supplies and straw bedding. The second room only contained more straw bedding.

Gabe stood in the doorway to the second room, watching Frank wander around the bodies.

Frank looked up. 'I've finished. We

need to get them to the cart.'

As Gabe strode forward, the animal carcasses hanging from the ceiling swayed. He gulped.

With a shared wince, Frank lifted the youngest boy's feet and Gabe lifted the shoulders. They carried him outside, his body leaving a snail's trail of blood, and laid him on the cart.

Ten minutes later thick hempen cloth covered four bodies on the back of the cart.

With his head hung Frank leaned on the cart and offered Gabe a cheroot.

'I feel queasy enough without that,' Gabe said.

'Yeah, me too,' Frank said with a hollow laugh. He pushed the cheroot back into his pocket and leapt on to the cart. 'Come on. I have to take them back to Carmon and organize a burial. And you have the rest of your family to meet.'

Gabe joined Frank in the cart. As they trundled towards Carmon, Gabe glanced back. In the back, a foot poked out from under the cloth.

'What will Devine do now?' Gabe asked with a gulp.

'He'll find Max and bring him in.'

Gabe stared straight ahead. 'Yeah, but who brings in Devine?'

3

The sun had set when Gabe and Frank reached the Cowie ranch.

Beside the neat fences, several carts and wagons pointed west. Splashes of colourful flowers trimmed the flat baked earth on the trail to the ranch. Beyond the perimeter, the fields of wheat and barley swayed in the breeze and the smaller vegetable-filled fields were in weed-free rows. A good mile from the ranch cowhands bustled around a mass of cattle, dusk-reddened dust funnelling into the sky.

Gabe alighted from the wagon and blew out his cheeks.

Frank slammed a hand on his back. 'Don't worry. This won't be too bad. We all want to see you.'

'How do they know I'm here?'

'I got word back before we went to Seth Randall's farm. Don't want the rest of the family being surprised — like I was.'

Gabe forced a smile. He climbed the long wooden steps and strode across the porch to the imposing oak front door of the two-storey house.

A young woman opened the door and Gabe grinned at her until he saw the maid's dress.

Frank slipped by Gabe and ushered him inside.

Gabe stepped into the marble-clad hall. Statues flanked the staircase, which swept away from him. Ornate doors lined the hall.

Gabe followed the maid through the third door on the right. Inside the room a smartly dressed man and a young woman stood surrounded by more furniture than had filled Gabe's whole home back in California.

The woman squealed and jumped on the spot. With a hitch of her skirts, she dashed to him and threw her arms around his neck.

Self-consciously, Gabe patted her

back. 'I'm guessing you're not a maid too.'

'I'm Thelma,' the woman mumbled, his shoulder muffling her voice.

Gabe wriggled from her grip and looked down at her.

'Howdy, Thelma. I'm Gabe.'

'Good.' She laughed. 'Hate to have hugged a new servant.'

She stepped aside as the man held out a hand.

'Billy McFadden,' he said, 'Thelma's beau.'

Gabe shook the thin hand. 'This is a friendly greeting.'

Thelma smiled. 'We're a right friendly family.'

To avoid more small talk, Gabe rocked back on his heels and glanced around the room, but so much furniture and ornaments were around him that his head spun.

'This is the largest home I've seen around these parts. How can anyone afford something like this?'

'Pa's done well . . . ' Thelma stepped

back, looking over Gabe's shoulder.

With a sickness in his stomach, Gabe turned. He faced an imposing gentleman. A trim white moustache nestled under his hollowed cheeks and wrinkles, the eyes cold reflective surfaces.

'You'd be my youngest?' Roy Cowie said.

'I am, sir.'

Roy nodded. 'Thelma, show him to his room. He'll need to freshen up. Dinner is at eight prompt.'

Roy turned and strode from the room. His footsteps echoed back down the hall, followed by a door slamming.

Gabe turned back to Thelma, who stared at her hands and fiddled with her dress.

'That's Pa,' she whispered.

Gabe shrugged. 'You'd better show me to my room then.'

★   ★   ★

Gabe had noted Thelma's ostentatious dress and Billy's neat suit, so he dressed in his best clothes. As he only had one change of clothing, this didn't require a difficult choice.

As the clock tinkled the hour, he shuffled his jacket closed and strode from his room. At the top of the staircase, he took a deep breath and paced down the sweeping staircase. Just as he reached the dining-room Frank and Thelma emerged from another room, followed by Billy.

'You're punctual,' Frank said, with a shake of his head. 'Is that the best you could do? You should have told me you didn't have a change of clothing. I could have lent you something.'

'I *have* changed.' Gabe worried his frayed sleeve. 'It's just . . . '

Thelma laughed and took his arm.

'My new brother looks just fine.' She led him into the dining-room. 'Are you courting? Because I have friends you might like to meet.'

Inside, Roy stared from the window. When Billy had shut the door, he turned and strode to the laid-out dining-table. He sat. With a crack of his right hand, he unfolded a napkin and swirled it on to his lap.

To Thelma's direction Gabe took a seat at the end of the table. He slipped the napkin off the table and sat on it. Then he leaned his elbows on the table and favoured everyone with a grin.

Roy tinkled a bell and everyone sat silently while the servants arrived with soup. They clattered the dishes on the table, Thelma and Frank directing operations with low voices, then left.

'Would you mind . . . ' Gabe coughed to clear a throat that felt smaller than it should be. 'Would you mind if I said grace?'

Roy flared his eyes, and Thelma gave a strangulated cry.

'You will not,' Roy snapped and spooned the soup into his mouth.

'Pa,' Frank said. 'If Gabe wants to

observe his traditions, we should honour them.'

Roy let his spoon clatter into his dish. He folded his arms.

'So, Martha filled your head with superstitious nonsense. Never had a need for it.'

'I ain't of a religious persuasion either,' Gabe said. 'But Ma always said there's nothing wrong with being thankful when you have good company and you have good food available.'

'I'll take that for your grace.' Roy snorted. He grabbed his spoon and returned to slurping his soup.

Gabe glanced at Frank, who shook his head.

Gabe shovelled his soup. The only sounds in the room were the clicking of spoons, the steady slurping, and the loud ticking of a clock.

When Gabe had had his fill of the thin soup, he pushed away the bowl and turned to Billy.

'What do you do, Billy?'

Billy dabbed at his mouth with his

napkin. 'I work for my father, but I'll soon be helping Mr Cowie.'

Thelma grinned. 'We'll all be seeing more of Billy soon.'

Frank chuckled. 'Not as much as some people will.'

'Frank, don't be rude.' Thelma chuckled. 'We have a guest.'

Billy slurped another mouthful of soup. 'What do you do, Gabe, when you ain't visiting family?'

'I'm a lawyer.'

Billy laughed. 'Might have guessed. Every generation of Cowie is a lawman. If I hadn't tamed Thelma, I'm guessing she'd have been — '

'Tamed!' Thelma shouted, swiping Billy across the arm with a resounding slap. 'You ain't tamed me.'

Roy tapped his spoon against his bowl.

'No raised voices at the table,' he murmured.

'Sorry, Pa.' Thelma turned to Gabe. 'How many bad men have you put away? Frank's been a sheriff for six months and they say his cells are the cleanest in the state. We don't get trouble.'

Frank pushed away his bowl and dabbed at his mouth.

'Plenty to be proud of there.'

Roy tinkled his bell and the silence returned as Frank and Thelma hung their heads.

Gabe stared over Roy's shoulder through the bevelled-glass window. The next course arrived accompanied by more low, polite directions from Thelma and Frank. When the servants had piled the beefsteak and vegetables on his plate and retired, Gabe noted that Thelma looked at him with her eyebrows raised.

Gabe considered their previous conversation and shook his head.

'I don't put away bad men. I ain't that sort of lawyer.'

'What sort are you?'

Before Gabe answered, Roy chuckled.

'Never had time for lawyers, no

matter what sort they are.'

Gabe forked a slice of beef into his mouth. He chewed and swallowed.

'Marshal Devine said as much to me earlier today.'

Roy speared a slice of beef. 'Then it must be right.'

Gabe slammed his fork into another slice of beef, then lifted his hand, leaving his fork sticking upright. He folded his arms.

'Carmon seems a mighty fine place. It's a testament to you, sir.'

Roy sneered. 'Don't patronize me.'

Thelma coughed. 'He ain't, Pa.'

'How do you know?' Roy muttered. 'Until an hour ago, you'd never talked to him.'

'But I have now and I'm glad that I have a fine, handsome brother.'

'What about me?' Frank said, laughing. 'Ain't I handsome enough?'

Thelma stuck out her tongue. 'Gabe and me got the Cowie good looks. You got what was left.'

'Enough!' Roy roared, his voice

rattling the glasses on the table.

Gabe picked up his knife and fork and resumed eating.

'Enough of what, Pa?' Frank whispered.

'This idle chatter.'

'Chattering idly is what families do at the dinner table.'

Thelma turned to Gabe. 'Never thought of that before. We are a family. Everybody that could be here, is here.'

Gabe put down his knife and fork. 'And I'm glad to be here.'

'And we're glad you're here.' She turned to Roy. 'Aren't we, Pa?'

Roy turned to Frank. 'I hear that Devine had some trouble out at Seth Randall's place.'

Frank glanced at Thelma. 'Yeah, that's why we were so late.'

'What happened?' Thelma asked and nibbled on a slice of beef.

'This ain't the place to discuss what happened.' Frank fingered his fluted glass, swirling the water round and sloshing it over the sides.

'Oh? Tell me,' Thelma said when she'd chewed her mouthful. 'What have the Randalls been doing now?'

Frank put down the glass and fiddled with his fork.

'What Frank ain't telling you,' Roy said, 'is that the Randall family is dead.'

Thelma gasped. 'All of them?'

'Yup,' Roy said while staring at Billy.

Thelma gulped and stared at the table. With a steady gesture, she slipped her hand towards Billy.

Billy placed his hands on the sides of his plate.

'You heard wrong,' Frank said. 'Devine didn't slaughter Max. He's still on the loose.'

With a whimper Thelma clasped both hands on her lap.

Roy snorted. 'I take it from your tone that you don't approve of Devine's approach.'

'No one can approve of what he did.'

'From what I hear, the worthless Randalls ambushed him and he took them in retaliation.'

'You've heard plenty in a short time.'

'I ain't a sheriff no more but I have my sources.' Roy leaned forward and waved his fork at Frank, freeing a dribble of meat juice. 'But you called in Devine to sort out the Randalls — seems like he's doing that.'

'*You* called for Devine. I approved your request. And you only asked him to bring in Max, not murder his family.'

'Me and Tor McFadden didn't make Carmon a place for decent people to live for the likes of the Randalls to destroy it.'

'Killing ain't the answer.'

With a lunge, Roy pushed back his half-eaten dinner. The plate spun to a stop, the food sprawling over the clean tablecloth.

'Don't be condescending to Devine. If it weren't for men like him, we wouldn't be sitting here with our fancy crockery and cloth on the table. Once, men like him stood between the pioneers and chaos.'

'You said it, Pa,' Frank said. 'Devine

43

did stand against chaos, but not any more. His time has passed and I ain't sad to see it gone.'

'Have respect, boy.' Roy slammed his fist on the table, knocking over his empty glass. 'People raised on soft living may judge Devine harshly, but I remember the early days and how life might have been.'

Frank sipped water and coughed. 'Don't excuse him killing four men — some almost children — because they were in his way.'

'Wrong! Four Randalls were in his way. They ain't men. Devine's here to do a job. Let him do it. A new lawman could learn plenty from him.'

'I learnt everything I need to know about the law from you.' Frank gulped the remainder of his water and poured another glassful from a large jug. 'And I'll do what I deem fit as sheriff.'

Roy leaned back in his chair and folded his arms.

'So, boy, what actions do you deem fit? You have a renegade Randall in the hills, who's never strayed far from the trading post and who ain't resourceful, even for a Randall. Then you have a lawman on his trail who's tracked down more men than even I have.'

'I can ride with Devine and ensure he does what I asked him to and bring Max in alive. Don't want him ensuring Max gets in the way and suffers the same fate as the rest of his family.'

Roy leaned back further. 'You can't take off when you please. It might take Devine a while to find Max. You can't leave Carmon undefended.'

'Why not?' Frank held his arms wide and glanced at the huge chandelier. 'As you keep telling me, the county's peaceful these days. Worst thing that's happened in the last month was Rock Watson getting drunk and breaking Ned Foster's store window. Carmon can look after itself while I'm with Devine.'

Roy clattered his chair back down. 'The law ain't about dealing with trouble when it happens. It's about letting the bad elements not make trouble in the first place. Your presence does that.'

'I can leave Deputy Wiles in charge while I'm gone.'

Roy smiled and Frank matched the smile.

'You could,' Roy said, 'but after supervision from Deputy Wiles, don't expect much of Carmon to be standing when you return.'

Frank chuckled and glanced at Gabe. 'What do you reckon, Gabe? Should I trust Devine to bring in Max?'

'If you doubt that a lawman can discharge his duties,' Gabe snapped, surprising himself with his sudden assurance, 'you should curtail his authority no matter what his record.'

'And that's what a fancy city lawyer reckons, is it?' Roy snapped.

'I ain't a criminal lawyer.'

'Like Thelma said — what other kind is there?'

'The kind that has a right to an opinion. Frank is Carmon's sheriff and you're the mayor. Between the two of you, I'd judge this to be Frank's concern.' Gabe noticed Frank suppress a smile by licking his lips.

'Wrong,' Roy shouted. 'We're both elected representatives but I represent people's aspirations and they want to live in peace. They don't care if the likes of the Randalls have their lives messed up. They just don't want them doing as they please and sniffing around their daughters.'

Thelma leapt to her feet.

'Permission to leave the table, Pa,' she whispered, with a whimper.

'No.' Roy pointed at her chair. 'Sit.'

Thelma sat and snuffled into a handkerchief.

Gabe took a deep breath. 'People want justice.'

'On that we can agree,' Roy said, 'but they want justice for themselves, not justice for the scum.'

'And who decides who the scum are?'

Roy grinned. With a finger raised, he leaned over the table.

'No,' Frank shouted. 'This ain't the time for *that* debate. This is Gabe's first night here. We shouldn't ramble on about town business.'

'That's all you ever do,' Billy mumbled and stared at his hands.

Roy snorted and fixed Frank with a hard stare.

'Then I'll end the discussion, boy. You ain't riding with Devine. Leave him to do his job and fetch Max, like we agreed.'

Frank stared back, then hung his head.

'He doesn't need to go,' Gabe said, without thinking. 'He can send his deputy.'

Roy smiled. 'You obviously ain't met Deputy Wiles. If Frank sent him out on his own, he'd never find his way back.'

Frank chuckled. 'That's something Pa and I never argue about.'

'I ain't saying Frank should send Deputy Wiles.' Gabe glanced around the room, noting the ticking clock, the servants loitering in the doorway, the

48

acres of crockery, his pa glaring at him ready to argue with anything he said. He smiled. 'He can send his new deputy, Deputy Gabe Cowie.'

As Frank smiled, Roy swept the bell to the floor. It rattled to the wall in a diminishing series of peals.

'But I'd love a tour of your home before I go,' Gabe said, turning to Thelma, 'if you wouldn't mind.'

4

'You made a mighty fine gesture last night,' Frank said when he and Gabe arrived at his office the next morning.

'It's no trouble for my new brother,' Gabe said.

Frank slammed a rifle and gunbelt with a Colt Peacemaker in the holster on his desk.

'Any preferred weapon? If these ain't suitable I can rustle up something else.'

Gabe slipped the gunbelt around his waist. 'This'll do.'

'Want a badge?'

'Just provisions and pointing in the right direction.'

Frank slipped a solid loaf from his larder and laid three strips of salted beef on it.

'After dinner last night I asked around. Devine took Uncas Jackson from the trading post and headed south

— probably to Monotony.'

Gabe slipped the food package into a saddle-bag and hoisted it over his shoulder.

'Any other advice for your new deputy?'

'Nope. I reckon that a Cowie will know what to do.'

Gabe bade Frank goodbye and rode from Carmon. He called in at the trading post and quizzed the bartender, but learnt nothing beyond what Frank had told him. Then he swung back on to the trail to Monotony.

To his surprise once he left Carmon, the trail was deserted. On either side scrubby vegetation clothed the low hills, but beyond that, thick forest enveloped the land. At times, the forest closed the trail to a well-trodden path through the trees.

At a steady trot, Gabe reached Monotony in late afternoon. From the saloon he learnt that Devine and Uncas had passed through three hours earlier, heading south.

Knowing he closed on Devine, he speeded, but when the sun approached the hills low cloud merged to fill the sky and persistent rain set in. The light dulled and so Gabe camped off the trail at the forest edge.

Although Gabe enjoyed hunting, he contented himself with warming his body beside a low fire while staying wrapped in his blanket. He chewed the hard bread and slices of beef that Frank had given him. With nothing to occupy his mind, he fell into a fitful sleep.

In the morning, he set off before daybreak. On the unfamiliar trail he made slow progress in the dark, but as the light expanded to fill the horizon, he speeded. Hoofprints peppered the trail, some fresh, some old.

He peered through the trees, searching for a camp-fire. Having set off so early, he ought to have gained on Devine, but if he'd passed him before Devine broke camp that mistake would take some unravelling.

When the sun poked above the trees,

Gabe worried that he might have made just that mistake and he spent as much time looking over his shoulder as examining the trail ahead. Then, framed against the sky on the crest of the next hill, he saw the unmistakable large outline of Devine, a smaller form riding hunched beside him.

Gabe spurred his horse to extra speed.

'Howdy, Marshal,' Gabe shouted when he reached the hilltop.

With a steady turn of his head, Jake glared back, but maintained his steady gait.

'You're that lawyer man. Howdy, I suppose. This is my new partner Uncas Jackson.'

Uncas frowned and tipped his hat. 'Gabe and I have met.'

Jake grinned. 'That explains Gabe's sour expression.'

Uncas grumbled and glared straight ahead.

'Are you making good time, Marshal?' Gabe asked.

'Yup. We're heading further south. If you're heading that way, you're welcome to ride along with us. Just don't expect us to wait for you.'

'Mighty kind.' Gabe sighed. 'But I'll be riding with you. Sheriff Cowie sent me. I'm his new deputy and he wants me to help you find Max.'

Gabe braced himself, but Jake kept his gaze fixed on the trail ahead.

'Uncas is the only help I need.'

Under his breath Uncas mumbled something indistinct.

'Sheriff Cowie reckons differently,' Gabe said. 'He ordered me to help you bring in Max.'

'Been a lawman for nigh on twenty-five years. I've had partners but never a deputy. So trot on back to Frank Cowie and tell him I'm fine.'

'I'll do that. But only when we have Max.'

Jake pulled his horse to a stop and swung it round. He leaned forward, his cold eyes fixing Gabe in a firm stare.

'How can a lawyer man help me?'

'I've met Max. I'm guessing you haven't. Knowing who you're looking for might help to reduce further . . .' Gabe shrugged, ' . . . misunderstandings.'

Jake rubbed his jaw. 'You guessed right, but that's why I have Uncas. He has all the recognizing skills I need.'

'Except Uncas is Max's friend. He can't be a reliable source of information.'

Jake glanced back at Uncas. 'You'd reckon so, but we have an understanding now. Ain't that so?'

Uncas rubbed his temple beside a large purpling bruise.

'Yup,' he mumbled.

'So, what else has a lawyer man to offer? Ain't got no use for courtroom debate or books of learning out here.'

'I can take care of myself.'

Uncas chuckled. 'He sure can. He helped me and Max give some McFadden boys a fair whupping.'

Jake raised an eyebrow. 'Did he? I can't see anyone helping a scrawny rat like you give someone a fair whupping. If he'd given *you* a whupping, I'd be more interested.'

Gabe sighed. 'So, where are we heading?'

'We are heading south. *You* are heading back to Carmon.'

Gabe slapped his saddle. 'You're wrong. Your orders are to find Max. My orders are to help you. They're both Sheriff Cowie's orders and we'll both follow them.'

Jake breathed through his nostrils and ruffled his beard as he appraised Gabe.

'Guessing Roy doesn't know you're here.'

'You guessed wrong. I agreed this with Mayor Cowie last night.'

Jake narrowed his eyes. 'I see. I forgot you claim you're a Cowie. So you're Roy's bastard, sniffing around for handouts with the other jackals.'

Gabe stared at the trail ahead, snaking down the hillside.

'I'm Roy and Martha Cowie's son,'

he said when his thudding heart slowed.

Jake chuckled. 'That ain't what I heard.'

'What you heard?' Gabe snapped.

'So, you reckon your claim to be a Cowie gives you the right to join me?' A slow smile spread across Jake's weathered face. His eyes opened wide. 'And I suppose it does. Roy and me rode together and had some fun. Suppose I have time for another Cowie to join me.'

Gabe bit his lip. 'Thank you kindly.'

Gabe encouraged his horse to a steady trot, but Jake stood still. Gabe pulled his horse to a halt and glanced over his shoulder.

'Remember,' Jake muttered, 'I'm in charge. We go when I say and stop when I say. You follow my orders or I'll give you a real whupping, not just the brawl you had with Uncas and Max.'

'That sounds fair.'

'I wasn't asking for an opinion.' Jake encouraged his horse to a steady pace.

Gabe filed in behind Jake and Uncas and they snaked down the trail.

After their initial conversation, neither Uncas nor Jake initiated further discussion, and Gabe saw no reason to either.

The trail continued to be deserted and as far as Gabe was concerned, unmemorable. He searched for landmarks but the scenery remained identical. On either side rolling hills clothed in forest stretched to the horizon, their trail a wide gap in the trees.

When the sun was high, they camped by a stream. Uncas watered their horses while they rested.

Gabe offered up the remains of his bread and beef.

Jake took a cut. With a long knife he cut the food into strips. Using a shorter knife he prodded a piece and chewed, his eyes never straying from the food until he'd consumed it. Then he mounted his horse and without a word, headed down the trail.

Gabe caught Uncas's eye. 'Guessing Jake ain't one for conversation.'

With his foot raised to the stirrup, Uncas glanced down the trail where Jake was fifty yards along. He rubbed his temple.

'Jake's good with conversation, but it's painful.'

Gabe filed in behind Uncas as they headed south.

The miles passed with monotonous regularity, and Gabe enjoyed the restful clump of his horse's hoofs. The sun warmed his face and the breeze was too slight to stir even the occasional open patches of scrubby grass that they passed.

As the afternoon wore on, he even became adept at spotting landmarks. He noted the occasional tree with its bark stripped — hills with peaks less rounded than other hills — streams that were wider than normal.

In the afternoon warmth, Gabe dozed as the trail snaked between two low hills.

A gunshot rang out.

Jake leapt from his horse. He knelt beside the trail and stared up the hillside at the forest.

Gabe shook himself from his torpor and swung from his horse. As Uncas dismounted and shuffled down behind a rock, he joined Jake, but kept his head low.

Jake narrowed his eyes, then leapt to his feet.

'Look after Uncas,' he said. 'I'll sort it out.'

Doubled-over, Jake sprinted for the trees. As he disappeared into the undergrowth, a man leapt up from behind a rock and dashed into the forest.

'Uncas,' Gabe said on a sudden whim, 'you ain't running while Jake's gone, are you?'

'And if I ran, do you reckon I'd get far before he got me?' To Gabe's headshake, Uncas shuffled round and sat back against the rock. 'So I ain't riling him more than needs be.'

Gabe glared at Uncas a moment, then leapt to his feet and dashed up the slope.

A minute after the man had headed into the trees, Gabe reached the forest. Their attacker had trampled a bush at the forest edge and Gabe paced over it, but he saw no other signs of the man's passage.

Gabe followed the direction the man had entered the forest and dashed through the trees. A dozen yards in, the forest darkened, but Gabe maintained his headlong dash.

A flash of a red bandanna through the trees rewarded his persistence.

Gabe kept his distance, ensuring he stayed far enough away for the man not to hear him, but close enough to follow.

A shot echoed through the trees and the man plummeted, clutching his shoulder. A second shot blasted, the man's gun wheeling from him.

In a blur, Jake emerged from a tangle of bushes. With a round-footed swipe, he kicked the man in the side.

The man rolled over twice.

Jake lifted his foot to kick him again.

'No,' Gabe shouted.

Jake flinched and swung his gun at Gabe.

'Never do that again,' Jake roared, aiming his gun back at the man. 'Most men who sneak up on me never sneak up on anything again.'

Gabe stopped twenty yards from Devine and pointed at the man.

'That ain't Max.'

'I was about to discover that for myself.' Jake narrowed his eyes. 'Thought I told you to guard Uncas.'

'Yeah. But I thought you might need my help.'

'I didn't, although you crashing through the trees might have alerted a cleverer quarry. Now get back to Uncas and stop that scrawny horse-thief from showing us his only skill.'

'You never said Uncas was a horse-thief.'

In a dismissive gesture Jake waved his arm.

'Ain't got time to tell you about everything you don't know. Now get, and get fast. I ain't wasting time tracking down Uncas too.'

With his head hung, Gabe turned and paced away, but as Jake didn't follow, he turned back.

Jake leaned down and grabbed the man's shirt.

'So, scum,' Jake roared, 'are you being co-operative or do you want to suffer?'

'Stop!' Gabe shouted.

Jake snorted and tumbled the prisoner down. He kicked him in the face and pointed at Gabe.

'Get back to Uncas, before you join this man in hell.'

Gabe backed a pace. He glanced at the fallen man, who rubbed an arm across his face, smearing the blood pouring from his nose. Gabe took deep breaths and glared at Jake.

'I ain't . . . ' Gabe flinched as the man rolled to his feet and dashed away.

Jake swivelled at the hip and, with a

contemptuous flick of his wrist, put a bullet in the man's back.

The man collapsed. As he lay, Jake blasted him twice more.

Jake swaggered to the man's side. He toed the man's ginger-haired head to one side, noting the slack expression. He chuckled and spat a huge gob of spit on the man's face.

'You picked the wrong man to fire at.'

'But you shot him in the back,' Gabe shouted.

'Don't tell me about the nobility of the gunfight,' Jake roared. 'Out here in the real world it's us against the scum. You remove them any way you can or end up with a bullet in your guts.'

Jake stormed away from the dead man, whistling under his breath. He brushed by Gabe, knocking him to his knees.

Gabe rolled to his feet and hurried on to walk beside Jake. 'Ain't you burying him?'

'Nope.'

'Did you recognize him or learn anything?'

'Nope.'

Gabe grabbed Jake's elbow and spun him to a halt.

'You might if you hadn't have killed him.'

'I didn't kill him.' Jake shrugged Gabe's hand from his arm. 'You killed him.'

Jake stormed through the trees and Gabe dashed after him. 'What's that mean?'

'It means my prisoner was ready to answer questions. Then you came along and scared him enough to run. I had no choice but to shoot him.'

Jake paused at the clearing and smiled.

Gabe followed Jake's gaze — Uncas still sat beside the trail.

'And will Max get the same leeway?'

'Nope.' Jake pushed the bushes aside. 'He'll get less.'

5

Jim, the bartender of the Silver Streak saloon, used a rare lull in custom to lean on the bar and sample a glass of his own brew. Tonight Monotony was full of people either passing through or enjoying the warm autumn evening and most of them wanted his services.

As he stretched, Mort Falcon wandered into the saloon and strode straight to the bar.

Jim smiled. 'What do you want?'

'Information.'

'Need a whiskey while you get it?'

'Yeah, but make it quick.'

'No trouble.' With practised skill, Jim poured a whiskey. 'The fastest whiskeys and the best information is what you'll get here.'

Mort took the offered glass and threw two coins on the bar.

'Got the first. I want the second. I'm

looking for Max Randall.'

Jim chuckled and pocketed the money.

'Max is all kinds of trouble,' he said, eking out the little he knew. 'He came through Monotony yesterday. He was in a hurry and had nothing but the clothes he stood up in, but he had money. He bought a change of clothes and a mess of provisions. Then he hightailed it out of here, all in half an hour. Didn't even stop for a whiskey.'

'Which way was he heading?'

'South.'

Mort knocked back his whiskey and tipped his hat.

Jim coughed. 'There's more.'

'Go on.'

'You ain't the only one after Max.' Jim licked his lips. 'Marshal Devine came through here looking for him, as did another man.'

'Was this man ginger-haired and about my height?'

'Nope — dark-haired and taller.'

'Name?'

Jim shrugged and Mort fished in his pocket for a dollar. Jim eyed the dollar, then shook his head.

'He gave no name and if people don't give them, I don't ask. Likewise I ain't remembering your name so that if someone asks, I can't tell.'

'You're a wise man.' Mort slipped the dollar on the table anyhow and Jim edged a hand on it.

'Thank you kindly.'

Mort slammed his hand on top of Jim's. 'Stay wise. I ain't been this way.'

'I understand,' Jim said, calculating the price he'd charge for information about him.

Mort turned and sauntered from the saloon.

Jim glanced outside and watched him saunter to his horse. A gaunt, white-haired man approached him and they chatted. Jim frowned, recognizing this man as Tor McFadden, the owner of Carmon's biggest ranch. Both men gesticulated to each other and mounted their horses. They trotted down the road, heading south, a further line of riders joining them to file past Jim's saloon doors.

Despite the warmth, Jim shivered and returned to his customers.

★　★　★

At sunset Devine's group camped beside a meandering river.

Jake hunted and bagged a rabbit, which they ate. Then they rolled into their blankets and slept without sharing a single word.

In the morning they rode off before daybreak and followed the trail south at a brisk pace.

Two hours after sunrise they crested the largest hill around. Being almost treeless, the hill gave them an uninter-rupted view of the forest for miles around. Below the trail split.

Jake stopped and, with a hand to his brow, he surveyed the hills.

'Any sign of Max?' Gabe asked.

'Nope.'

Jake bunched his reins and headed down the right-hand trail. An hour later the trail split again and this time Jake took the left-hand trail.

Gabe hurried after him. 'Are you following any particular track of hoof-prints, or are you just guessing?'

Jake glared back at Uncas until Uncas shuffled round to stare back.

'I'm following Uncas.'

Uncas grunted, but as Jake continued to stare at him, he waved an arm at Jake.

'Then you're a fool. I'm just following *you* until you tell me I don't have to any more.'

'And I won't let you go until you lead me to Max.'

Uncas returned to staring at the ground before his horse.

When Jake turned too, Gabe shuffled his horse closer to Uncas.

'Uncas, do you know where Max is heading?' he asked.

'Nope. I keep telling the big man, but he ain't listening.' Uncas rubbed the yellowing bruise on his temple. 'And I don't fancy trying to make him listen again.'

From ahead, Jake chuckled. 'Don't believe a word that scrawny horse-thief tells you.'

Gabe sighed. 'Uncas, tell me what you know.'

'Why should I? You're a lawman, like Devine.'

'I'm a lawman, but I ain't like Devine. I sided with you in the trading post. I saved you a beating then, and if you trust me, I might save you from another beating.'

'If you could save me a beating, I'd be grateful, but as I don't know anything about Max's whereabouts, that ain't happening.'

Gabe waved at the trail, which stretched ahead until it disappeared into the trees.

'But you know that Max headed south.'

'Yeah, but . . . '

Jake laughed and turned in the

saddle. 'And that's why I'm following him. He knows more than he's letting on and he ain't returning to Carmon until he tells me the truth.'

Gabe fixed Uncas with his most honest stare.

'Trust me. Tell me what you know and I'll let you go.'

Uncas glanced over Gabe's shoulder at Jake.

'The big man won't accept that.'

From ahead, Jake grunted.

'Tell me the truth,' Gabe said. 'I'll worry about him.'

Uncas sighed. 'All Max said was that he was heading south.'

'When did he tell you this?'

'Just before he headed south.'

'Smart answers just make me think Devine is right about you.' Gabe turned from Uncas and hurried ahead.

'He told me that after you left the trading post,' Uncas shouted after him.

Gabe slowed to let Uncas catch up with him. 'When I left, Max had gone.'

'Yeah, but he returned.' Uncas

glanced at Devine and gulped. 'He was desperate. Devine had killed his family. I gave him money and directed him to Monotony and the trail south. That's it.'

'That don't sound right. I've never been to these parts before, but I didn't need many directions to Monotony and beyond.'

'Perhaps I should invent something, because that's the truth.'

Gabe hurried on to draw alongside Jake. 'Why do you reckon there's more, Jake?'

'Because I know scum like Uncas. He wouldn't give a dying man a dime to buy his last drink.' Jake spat on the ground. 'He'd steal a dime from a dying man though.'

'Uncas ain't as bad as you think.'

Jake snorted. 'Ask yourself one thing — why would Uncas give money to Max?'

'He's my friend,' Uncas whined before Gabe answered. 'We help each other and he'd do the same for me.'

A slow chuckle escaped Jake's lips. 'And there it is. Scum like Uncas don't give money away without any hope of seeing it again. That fact doesn't stack up and when it does, I'll let Uncas go.'

Uncas slammed a fist on his saddle, and Gabe leaned back to flash him a sympathetic smile.

'So, Uncas,' Gabe said, 'as you'll be with us for a while, which way should we go?'

'I ain't leading,' Uncas murmured, waving an arm down the trail. 'I'm at the back.'

'Yeah,' Jake said, 'in everything.'

Around noon, Gabe's worries that they were heading in the wrong direction lessened when they passed a wagon train heading north.

Jake questioned the wagon leader and received a description of a blond-haired man he'd seen earlier that day who just had to be Max.

An hour after meeting the wagon train, Gabe rode up alongside Jake.

'As we're closing on Max, what are

we doing when we reach him?'

Jake snorted. 'I take him in.'

'I've no doubt that Max won't be a match for the legendary lawman Marshal Jake T. Devine, but how do you take an armed man alive when he don't want to be taken?'

'Sarcasm is lost on me, lawyer man.'

'I wasn't being sarcastic. Sheriff Cowie's orders are to take Max alive and a man who's run this far ain't wanting that, so what can you do?'

In response, Jake just grinned with a wide arc of yellow teeth.

Uncas laughed. 'You ain't talking Devine's language. He doesn't waste one second's thought on how to capture a man. He only knows how to bring them back with a bullet in their forehead.'

Gabe nodded. 'Uncas's right, Jake. So when we close on Max, I'll take him in.'

'You what?' Jake roared, swirling round in the saddle.

Gabe glared back at Jake, meeting his

eyes with a level gaze.

'We have our orders.'

Jake turned first. 'We have, and when you've faced as many scum as I have, you can tell me what to do. Until that day comes, stay out of my way.'

'Can't do that,' Gabe said with his voice low. 'Max will have a fair trial and that's more justice than your version of the law will give him.'

'Wrong, lawyer man. He can die with a gun in his hand and his dignity intact, instead of swinging from a noose in Carmon.'

From behind, Uncas coughed.

'As you're set for a big argument,' Uncas said, 'perhaps we should stop and sort this out.'

'We ain't,' Jake muttered and nodded forward.

Gabe followed Devine's gaze. Ahead, about 500 yards, a man rode down the hill. Although he was too far away to recognize, blond hair stuck out from beneath his hat.

'Max,' Jake muttered.

★ ★ ★

When Sheriff Frank Cowie returned from his early evening stroll around the ranch, he stopped in the hall and glanced through the open door of the living-room.

Roy sat in his chair, staring through the window, looking west. Frank tapped on the door. He received no response but sauntered inside.

'Evening, Pa.'

'Evening, boy,' Roy murmured, turning from the window. 'Anything on your mind?'

'I'm wondering what you're made of Gabe.'

Roy snorted and stared through the window.

Frank stood a moment. He turned to leave. Then he turned back.

'Pa, why did you send Devine after Max Randall?'

Roy stared up at him, his face a blank mask in the half-light.

'Ah, *that* question.'

As the silence stretched, Frank heard the clock tick.

'I ain't asking about Ma, or about Gabe, or about all the other things I know you don't want to answer, but this ain't a family question. It's a Carmon question, and as sheriff I need to know.'

'A sheriff shouldn't need to ask.'

'Do you mean that I should know what's happening without being told?'

Roy chuckled and leaned back in his chair. 'That's as good an answer as any. You can't rely on me now to tell you what to do. Show initiative and find things out for yourself.'

Frank paced to the chair opposite to Roy and ran his hands along the chair back.

'Max was mouthing off, saying you and Tor McFadden are no good and that Carmon's folk should run you both out of town. That was a stupid demand.'

'It was.'

'But no man deserves having Devine

chasing him down for stupidity. We can sort that out ourselves.'

'We could and we should, but we won't. Devine will produce the truth. He always does.' Roy turned to the window.

Frank said his goodbyes and paced from the room and up the sweeping stairs. At the step where he could see into the living-room, he glanced at Roy who still stared through the window, then continued up the stairs.

As Frank passed Thelma's room, he heard crying. He backtracked, wavered a moment, then knocked on her door.

Inside, Thelma snuffled. Footsteps padded to the door.

'Who is it?' she asked.

'It's Frank. Can I come in?'

Dressed in her night-gown Thelma opened the door and, for the first time for years, he entered her bedroom.

Frank glanced at her tear-stained cheeks. Today, Billy had headed off and he could guess the rest.

'I've been talking with Pa,' he said.

'There's a first time for everything. Did you ask him about Gabe?'

'I tried, but he said nothing.'

Thelma snuffled. 'That's to be expected, but I'm guessing Pa was pleased to see him.'

Frank laughed and sat on the bottom of the bed. 'That's a big guess. They just argued.'

With her night-gown wrapped about her, Thelma slipped under the blankets and sat in her bed.

'You've suffered enough family meals to know that one was different. We talked. It wasn't agreement, but Billy said that the discussion was much more like a normal family meal.'

'It'd be nice to be a normal family.'

Thelma picked at her night-gown. 'When Gabe returns, do you reckon he'll stay long enough for us to get to know him? I know he went after Devine to escape from the atmosphere, but I'd hate for him to stop trying.'

'I don't reckon Gabe is in a hurry to reach New York and I'm sure we'll get to know each other enough to stay in touch. Whatever happens, we've your wedding next year to invite him back for and things are sure to be easier the second time.'

'They couldn't be worse.' Thelma buried her head in her hands and sobbed. She threw back her head and opened her eyes wide. A tear dribbled down her face and she brushed it from her cheek.

'Has Billy gone for long?'

'Billy?'

'Yeah, Billy. He left today on business.'

'Oh, yeah . . . I don't know.' Thelma snuffled back another sob. 'He keeps saying the next time will be the last, but it never is. Whatever happens, it won't be long before he won't go again.'

'Good. It'll be nice when we're always a family.'

Thelma giggled and glanced away. 'Pa said as much last week. He's anticipating the next line of Cowies, except mine will be a McFadden. So we'll have to wait until you're wed.'

'But do you think Pa will ever tell us about Ma?'

Thelma pursed her lips. 'He will when he's ready.'

'We've waited for twenty years. If he don't tell us while Gabe's here, he never will.'

Thelma shuffled under the blankets. 'You've spent more time with Gabe. Did he say anything about why they left?'

'No. We didn't have a relaxing time before we came to the ranch — what with the bodies.'

Thelma gulped and glanced away. 'Guess not.'

'But despite the situation, it was nice spending time together.'

'Don't suppose there's an easy way to ask.'

'Sure ain't. We want to know. Gabe wants to know. But the only ones who can tell us are either dead or won't say anything.'

'I was right before.' Thelma picked at

a frayed edge of her blanket. 'Gabe and I have the Cowie good looks and you have the Cowie good sense.'

Frank laughed. 'I'll let that insult go, but from what I've seen of Gabe, I reckon we both have the Cowie good sense.'

Thelma echoed the laugh. 'And I'll ignore your insult, but it rules out my theory.'

'Theory?'

'When Gabe wrote last year, I said the most likely explanation was . . . ' Thelma coughed, 'was that our pa ain't Gabe's pa. A young woman wouldn't head to California with a week-old baby without good reason. Pa's tough, but sending her away like that . . . He had to have a reason, and the child being someone else's seems the only possibility to me.'

Frank stared at his hands. 'But that only leaves the Randalls.'

Thelma picked at her frayed blanket, tangling away a loose thread and wrapping it around her finger.

'We've argued for too many years with them.'

'Grandpa once told me that Seth and Pa were friends.'

Thelma snapped off the piece of thread and folded her hands across her belly.

'Either way,' she said, snuffling, 'Pa's hatred of the Randalls is closer to home.'

Frank saw a new potential for waterworks and rose from the bed.

'I'll leave you. It's late.'

Thelma pulled the blankets up to her chin. 'Take care, Frank. I reckon things will be hard on us all soon.'

Frank almost leaned down to kiss his sister's forehead, but decided not to and walked to the door.

6

On reaching the spot where they'd seen Max, Jake Devine dismounted and knelt beside Max's prints. Then he leapt back on his horse.

'Why check his prints?' Gabe asked. 'We can see him.'

'I might lose sight of him,' Jake snapped. 'But once I have his prints, I'll never lose him.'

Jake shook the reins and continued at the same sedate pace as before.

'Why not speed up? Then we won't lose sight of him?'

'Can see you ain't tracked anyone before. You do nothing to perturb your quarry until you're closer.' Jake smiled. 'Then you do plenty of perturbing.'

At the next hilltop, they had gained on Max, but he had ridden from the trail.

With his hand to his brow, Gabe

gazed along Max's future route — he was heading to a collapsed shack by the trail.

Jake pointed. 'And that's why we don't hurry. We have him where we want him.'

Gabe glanced to the sky, judging they had another hour before sunset.

Just down from the crest they settled and, as darkness began to shroud the land, on foot they edged down the slope to the shack. A night chill enveloped them when they reached the bottom of the slope. Around them, the trees were mere outlines.

Max's fire lit the shack's fragmented walls as he edged back and forth, collecting wood and making camp.

They hunkered down out of range of the firelight.

'Look after Uncas,' Jake said. 'Keep him quiet. And this time, do it.'

Gabe glanced back at the docile Uncas. 'Shall I gag him?'

'No need.' Jake patted Uncas's shoulder. 'After one word, your friend dies. Understand?'

As Uncas nodded, Jake turned.

'Max!' Uncas roared and leapt to his feet. 'Watch out!'

Jake swirled round. With the back of his hand he clubbed Uncas across the cheek for him to fall.

Uncas pushed to a sitting position. 'We *do* have an understanding.'

'Uncas, is that you?' Max shouted from the shack.

Jake pulled Uncas to his feet and leaned his face down to peer into Uncas's eyes. He pulled his fist back, then turned to spit on the ground.

'Ain't got time to knock you into oblivion. You've told him we're here, so finish the job. Let him know the situation.'

Jake swung Uncas round to stand before him. When Uncas snorted, Jake kicked him on the back for him to stumble forward.

'It's me,' Uncas shouted. He cleared his throat. 'I have company.'

In the derelict shack Max held a

hand to his brow and lifted a foot on to the short, collapsed wall.

'Come on in,' he shouted. 'I have a fire going.'

'Marshal Devine and a deputy are with me.'

Max leapt behind the wall.

'You idiot,' he shouted.

Jake chuckled. 'Your friend talks sense.'

'I'm sorry,' Uncas shouted. 'Devine didn't give me a choice.'

'Yeah,' Jake shouted. He paced forward and clubbed Uncas out of the way. 'And I ain't giving you a choice either. Come out.'

Jake dropped to his haunches and levelled his gun over his arm.

'Assume you're giving me the same choices as you gave my family?' Max shouted, with only the top of his hat visible over the short wall.

'You're a smart man.'

Gabe dropped to his knees and shuffled forward to kneel beside Jake.

'I thought you were giving him a

chance?' Gabe said.

'Just speaking in terms he'll understand.'

A gunshot echoed in the night and Gabe dropped to his belly. He glanced to his side. Jake was already on his belly.

'This wasn't inevitable,' Gabe snapped. 'You forced him to fire.'

Jake rolled on to his back and flexed his shoulders. He glanced up at his gun and rolled the barrel.

'Twenty years ago, me and Roy Cowie holed up for five days sniffing a bunch of scum from a shack like this one. When they came out, we were waiting.'

'Don't suppose they lived?'

Jake winked and rolled on to his front again. With his forearms planted in a firm triangle, he levelled his gun at the shack.

Max fired again. This time the shot whistled scant feet over Gabe's head.

'Keep your head down, lawyer man,' Jake whispered, 'and you'll be fine.

Just watch and learn how this is done.'

'Don't fancy learning how to kill a man, but I'd like to see you take him alive. That'd take skill.'

With an eye closed, Jake adjusted his stance. 'I stick with what works.'

Gabe rolled to his side. 'Why won't you try to arrest Max?'

Jake shuffled his stance down further.

'How old do you think I am?' he asked, keeping his gaze on the shack.

In the sallow light from Max's fire, Gabe glanced at Jake's face. Years of grime and outdoor living weathered the cheeks.

'What's that matter?'

'I'm about as old as your pa and I'm a lawman. You don't see many old outlaws or old lawmen. We live by the bullet and that's how we die. Those that get old follow a simple creed. They never take chances. One piece of ill luck or mistake and you're dead. I take no chances. I'm alive.'

'*I* am prepared to take a chance.'

Gabe shuffled up to a crouch.

Jake waved an arm forward. 'Be my guest. Get yourself killed if you want to.'

'Thought you'd want to protect the son of your old friend?'

'Nope. Roy's pa never protected Roy and he won't want to protect his sons either. You'll learn either to not act reckless or end up dead.'

Gabe rolled to his feet and stood between the shack and Jake.

'Max,' he shouted. 'I'd like to talk to you.'

'Talk away,' Max hollered.

'I'll walk towards you. I've holstered my gun.'

From behind Gabe, Jake snorted.

'Start praying Max is a poor shot,' he muttered.

Gabe lifted his hands to shoulder level. As he edged towards the side of the collapsed wall, Max appeared, crouched behind the wall.

'That's close enough, lawman,' Max said.

Gabe held his arms higher. 'I'm a lawman, but you know me as Gabe.'

Beneath his hat, Max narrowed his eyes. 'You are the man from the trading post.'

'Yeah. And if you remember, you and I fought on the same side.'

'I remember, but I also remember that you wouldn't take a drink from me.'

Gabe relaxed his stance. 'I didn't like what you'd been saying. But I dealt with you fairly then and I'll deal with you fairly now.'

Max knelt beside the wall but kept his gun on Gabe.

'What do you want?'

'I want you to throw down your gun.' Gabe took another pace forward. 'Then I want to take you back to Carmon, alive.'

'You want a lot.' Max laughed and gestured with his gun over the wall. 'But I guess the big man doesn't share your view.'

Gabe glanced back at Jake whose

head-on form was barely visible in the dark.

'I know he's serious about bringing you in.'

'He killed my pa and brothers. Do you reckon I'm surrendering to him?'

'I ain't asking you to surrender to him.' Gabe took another pace forward. 'I'm asking you to surrender to me.'

Max firmed his gun hand. 'Surrendering to Roy Cowie's son is as bad.'

'A man who fought on your side doesn't deserve that attitude.'

Max edged to the end of the wall. From five yards away he stared up at Gabe. He nodded.

'Perhaps you're right. But I ain't resting until Devine pays for what he did. So stand aside and let me and Devine sort this.'

'You heard the man,' Jake shouted. 'He's talking more sense than you is and more sense than his worthless family did.'

With an angry oath, Max aimed his gun over the wall.

Gabe dashed forward.

'No!' he shouted.

Max aimed his gun up at Gabe, his eyes bright. 'Get back, lawman.'

With his arms raised again, Gabe stood his ground.

'If you don't give yourself in, you'll die. But if the charges against you ain't serious, you can sort them out and be free.' Gabe lowered his voice to a whisper. 'Then long after this is over, Jake will be sitting by his camp-fire and you can be in the bushes with a gun trained on him.'

'You speak sense, but the second I stand up, Devine will kill me.'

'He will if you have a gun, but throw it down and he won't — not while I'm here.'

Max hung his head and stared at his gun. Without looking up, he underhanded it towards Gabe.

'Make sure I don't regret this.'

Gabe paced into the firelight and grabbed the gun. He turned as Jake strode by him and loomed over Max, a foot raised on the wall.

'You heard my promises, Jake,' Gabe said.

Jake glanced at the sky. 'Then it's time for food. I'll be back later. Guard our prisoners.'

Jake stalked into the gathering night. Long after he'd gone Max glared after him.

As ordered, Gabe guarded Max and Uncas, who sat on opposite sides of the fire. They stared at the flames and the smoke pluming into the sky.

When full darkness arrived Jake returned and they cooked and ate the two birds that he'd caught.

'You idiot, Uncas,' Max muttered, then spat out a bone.

'You have me wrong,' Uncas said. 'I told Devine nothing.'

'You didn't need to. You just led him to me.'

'I didn't.' Uncas jumped to his feet and stamped his right boot. 'Devine asked in the saloon in Monotony. The bartender said you headed south and we came upon you in this shack.'

'Yeah, I'm sure.'

Jake chuckled. 'I've chased conniving outlaws across the most unforgiving territories and you ain't a patch on the stupidest of them. I could have found you even without Uncas's help.'

'I didn't help,' Uncas whined. 'I never told you where Max would be.'

With his head thrown back, Jake laughed. 'For the last two days you've said you knew nothing, except you're now saying that you *did* know where he was. I'd stay quiet if I were you.'

Uncas mumbled to himself.

'Why bring Uncas?' Gabe asked. 'You knew how to find Max.'

'I needed his help.' Jake rolled to his haunches and with a great swipe, cuffed Uncas's shoulder. 'Ain't that so, scum?'

Uncas opened his mouth, then closed it and threw himself to the ground. He hugged his knees.

'That ain't it,' Gabe said. 'You're just a bully, who needs someone to beat.'

'You have me wrong, lawyer man. I

followed where Uncas led.'

Uncas slapped his thigh. 'Stop saying that! I led you nowhere. I was at the back the whole time.'

'Only so we wouldn't have to look at your ugly hide.'

Gabe sighed. 'We have Max. You don't need to abuse Uncas any more — just tell us how he led you to Max.'

Jake sauntered from the fire and busied himself with checking his rigging. When he'd finished he stood beside his horse with his hands on his hips.

'As you want to be a lawman, I'll tell you. Uncas was born in Waltersville. He still has folks there. When Max headed south, that's where he'd go. I needed Uncas to fish him out when we got there, but we found him on the way.'

Gabe glanced at Uncas, who hung his head even more. 'How did you know where Uncas was born?'

'I told him,' Uncas whispered.

Jake grinned. 'See, Max? Your friend's an idiot.'

Max stood and held out a hand. 'Now I've heard the truth, I ain't holding a grudge.'

Uncas took the hand and Max pulled him to his feet. While still smiling, Max clubbed Uncas's jaw with his left hand.

Moving like lightning, Jake surged three long paces and slammed both fists on Max's back. As Max slumped, Jake kicked him in the side. Max rolled to receive another firmer kick to the chest.

'Jake,' Gabe shouted. 'That's enough.'

'Why? Max has to know just how far he can go, and hitting Uncas is too much.' Jake grinned. 'It's my job to pulp his scrawny hide.'

'He didn't mean anything,' Uncas whined, dashing to Max's side. 'We're always fighting. That's how we sort our differences.'

Jake raised his fist. 'Max ain't sorting his differences with anyone, not when he's under my charge.'

As Max glared up at Jake, Gabe paced between them.

'You ain't mistreating our prisoner,' he snapped.

'*We* have no prisoner. *I* have a prisoner.'

'I'm Sheriff Cowie's deputy. So *we* have a prisoner and *you* ain't mistreating him.'

'Whatever you say, Sheriff Cowie's deputy.'

Without further word, Jake rolled into his blanket for the night.

With the argument petering out, Gabe's enthusiasm abated, so he left Jake to do whatever he felt was necessary and slept.

The next morning they rose at dawn. To barked instructions from Jake, they mounted their horses. Jake tethered Max's horse to his, but to Gabe's surprise he didn't bind Max's wrists. Then they headed back on to the trail, but Jake swung his horse to the south.

'Where are we going?' Gabe shouted as he swung round to follow Jake.

'There's a trail through the forest ten miles on.'

'Is it quicker?'

'Nope, but I never return the same way. If you do that, you meet whoever is following you.'

Gabe stared back over his shoulder. 'We're being followed?'

'No idea. Don't intend to find out, either.'

For an hour they rode in sullen silence, until Jake swung his horse from the southern trail and headed for the forest.

With a glance at each other, the others followed, but as they closed on the forest, a thin trail opened. They bent as they entered the forest and broke through the trees for 300 yards before they joined a wider northern trail.

For the rest of the day they rode in silence, only resting at noon to water their horses.

That evening, they pulled up in a clearing by a meandering stream and to Jake's instructions, Uncas gathered wood. Then Max and Uncas sat back from the stream, staring away from each other, each with their legs drawn up — Jake still didn't bind Max.

Wispy clouds filled the sky, the setting sun shrouding them in arcs of redness, promising a crisp, cold night to come.

Gabe lit the fire, although the greener wood Uncas had collected meant it produced more smoke than heat.

Jake sauntered around the fire. With his heel, he scuffed the dirt, marking a circle. When he'd finished, he strode back to the fire.

'I've set out our area,' he said. 'Anyone who strays outside that circle ain't got a good reason and will answer to me.'

Max chuckled and shuffled closer to the fire. 'What if we want privacy in the bushes?'

'You have no reason to go in the bushes. Inside this circle will do just fine.'

'Thanks,' Max and Gabe murmured simultaneously.

Uncas snorted and stood on the circle edge, near to his horse, staring east.

'What's on your mind, scum?' Jake muttered.

'Just wondering how far it is to Monotony.'

Jake glanced around at the darkening forest. 'About ten, twelve miles.'

'Thought so. Reckon I might take off there.'

'And why are you reckoning that?'

'I'm no use to you any more and Max could do with time away from me.'

Max nodded. 'Yeah. I'll see you later, Uncas.'

Uncas tipped his hat to Gabe. 'Can't say it's been fun riding with you.'

'Take care,' Gabe said.

Uncas turned to his horse and strode over the scuffed line Jake had marked.

'You're going nowhere,' Jake roared.

Uncas stopped beside his horse. 'I was only travelling back with you because we're going in the same direction. But if I want to visit

Monotony and find better company, that's my decision.'

Jake slipped his gun from its holster. 'Your decision doesn't matter. Come back inside my circle or I'll drag you back in feet first.'

Uncas glanced at the gun and edged inside the circle.

'You could hold me when you were searching for Max. You had no cause but I couldn't argue. That's changed.'

'Nothing's changed for you, scum.'

'Uncas's right,' Gabe said. 'We don't need him.'

'Can't see anyone ever needing Uncas, but he's still going nowhere.'

As Jake raised his gun, Gabe paced round to stand between them.

'Why? Uncas ain't under arrest. We don't need to keep him.'

Jake narrowed his eyes. 'Uncas stays because I want him to stay.'

'That ain't a reason. Put away that gun, Marshal.'

'Or what?' Jake muttered, keeping his gaze on Uncas.

Gabe let his threat go unvoiced and a smile spread on Jake's face. Moving slowly, Jake holstered his gun and folded his arms.

Uncas nodded to Gabe. With the barest glance at Jake, he turned.

As Uncas's foot paced beyond the circle again, Jake leapt at him. With lightning speed, he slammed his fist into Uncas's cheek.

Uncas collapsed and rolled twice, stopping outside the circle.

'Either stay down,' Jake roared with his fist high, 'or get up and let me hit you again.'

Uncas rolled to a sitting position and stared up at Jake.

'You can't treat me like this, Marshal. I've done nothing and I ain't under arrest.'

Jake bunched his fist tighter, his face gleaming. 'Keep on speaking, scum. Give me a reason to knock sense into you.'

From behind Jake Max leapt to his feet and took a running jump on to

Jake's back. He wrapped both hands around Jake's neck, but with a casual gesture, Jake drove his elbow into Max's guts.

As Max staggered back, Jake swung round and grounded him with an uppercut to the chin. He stood over him a moment but Max's head lolled back. Jake swirled round to face Uncas and spat on his fist.

'Ready for the same treatment, scum?'

Gabe stormed across the campsite to Jake. He slammed a hand on his shoulder and swung him round.

'Stop this,' he shouted.

Jake's eyes blazed. He stared at the hand on his shoulder until Gabe lifted it.

'Got no reason to explain myself to a deputy, but as you asked so nicely, I'll teach you about the law. Uncas helped Max escape and that's a crime. He has questions to face back at Carmon and I'll make sure he answers them.'

Gabe glanced away. 'That's as maybe,

but you got no reason to hit him.'

'Gives me all the reasons I need.'

Uncas stood and batted the dust from his clothes.

'I'll stay with you and return if that's what Devine wants.' Uncas glared at Jake. 'Sheriff Cowie won't detain me that long. Then I'll be free to join Max. Guess who'll be the first person we'll search for?'

Jake spat on Uncas's boots. 'Do I look scared, scum?'

Uncas grunted and backhanded his fist towards Jake's face.

With a lightning gesture, Jake swung his hand up, catching Uncas's fist inches from his face. He gripped Uncas's hand and thrust it down and back, spinning Uncas round to thrust his arm half-way up his back.

'Get off, Marshal,' Uncas whined.

'You attacked a lawman. That's another crime. You'll never get out of jail to do any searching.'

Uncas gasped as Jake drove his hand up, pushing him on to his tiptoes to avoid having his arm wrenched from its socket.

'Don't matter how long it takes, Marshal, I'll find you.'

'I'm already looking forward to it,' Jake muttered into Uncas's ear.

'Enough, Jake,' Gabe shouted. 'Uncas's going nowhere. Put him down.'

'He ain't sorry he attacked me yet.'

'I am. I am,' Uncas shouted, trying to kick his legs back while keeping his balance.

Jake threw Uncas down. 'Is that enough, Gabe?'

Gabe glanced at the floundering Uncas. He nodded.

Jake kicked Uncas on the shin.

'And is that enough?' he roared.

'Stop,' Gabe muttered, taking a pace towards Jake.

Jake booted Uncas squarely on the chin for him to land two yards back.

'Is that enough?'

Gabe rolled his weight forward, ready to leap at Jake, but reason defeated the blood coursing through his veins. He sighed.

'If I have to say that you're in charge to stop you hurting Uncas, I'll say it.'

'So say it,' Jake spat.

'You're in charge.'

'And the rest.'

'It ain't enough until you say so.'

'If you insist.' Jake stormed to Uncas. He hauled him to his feet and with an ironlike fist punched him deep in the guts.

Uncas folded over the fist, then staggered away, retching bile over his boots.

Jake patted his hands together. 'Now that's enough.'

'It ain't,' Uncas roared, righting himself. He spat on the ground and charged Jake. He wrapped both arms around Jake's chest and pushed him backwards, tumbling him down.

Jake scrambled back and rolled on to his front.

With a great roar, Uncas leapt on Jake's back. He grabbed his hair and slammed his face into the dirt.

As Gabe drew his gun, Uncas punched Jake in the kidneys.

But Jake surged up, bucking Uncas from his back. As he lifted he grabbed Uncas around the neck. He dropped to his knees, holding Uncas's neck in a stranglehold.

'That wasn't a smart thing to do, scum.'

In a sudden gesture Jake grabbed Uncas's chin with his left hand. He thrust his hand to the side. A sickening crack echoed through the clearing as Uncas slumped, his head at an angle to his body.

Gabe closed his eyes. A gunshot sounded and he opened them.

Jake stood over Uncas, a flurry of smoke rising from his gun, a neat whole in Uncas's forehead.

'You didn't need to do that,' Gabe muttered. 'You'd already killed him.'

'He might have had some life in him.' Jake spat on Uncas's face. 'I did him a favour with the bullet.'

'Is that more of your law?'

Jake swung his Peacemaker into its holster. 'Don't know any other kind.'

Jake hunkered down beside the fire and whistled tunelessly through his teeth.

7

In the cold heart of the night, Gabe scuffed a clear area beside the trees and collected rocks.

The noise woke Max and he went to Uncas. With his head hung, he knelt over his friend's body, then stood, avoiding catching Jake's eye, and walked to Gabe. When he reached the circle edge, he lifted his leg high and strode over it.

Gabe tensed, but Jake turned and strode to his horse, whistling. He unstrapped his rifle, loaded it, and stalked into the night.

Still in silence, Gabe and Max collected rocks from further afield and piled them around Uncas's body.

To Max's agreement, Gabe said some words that his ma had taught him. They stood, heads bowed, then returned to the fire, where Jake was wolfing through one of the rabbits he'd caught while they were burying Uncas.

Gabe took the other rabbit, divided it, and passed the half-carcass to Max. He sat cross-legged and chewed through the stringy meat, keeping his gaze on the fire.

'My family,' Max said, 'now Uncas — am I next, Marshal?'

Jake fingered the rabbit carcass remnants, then threw it into the fire and wiped his sticky fingers on his jacket. With a spare branch, he stoked the fire — smoke funnelled and the fire settled into a solid burn.

'Doubt anyone could care about the Randall family.' Jake folded his arms. 'They were as worthless as Uncas was.'

Gabe glared at the fire, gritting his teeth, but as Jake threw a log on the fire, he saw that Max looked at him with raised eyebrows.

'Be quiet, Max,' Gabe snapped. He fiddled away another scrap of meat from his carcass, then hurled it into the fire. 'Any more food, Jake?'

Jake backed from the fire. 'Nope, but we've had more to eat since we removed Uncas's worthless hide. We'd have even more to eat if I didn't have to feed Max.'

Jake lifted his left foot to swing a kick at Max.

'What?' Max shouted. He rolled from a kick that didn't come.

With his foot drawn back Jake roared his laughter.

'Now that's the sort of prisoner I like — one who knows his place. As a reward, I'll only kick you the once.'

'You ain't mistreating Max,' Gabe shouted, leaping to his feet.

Jake placed his foot back on the ground. 'I tried to teach Uncas a lesson but he wasn't bright enough to understand. Max is cleverer — not that that's a compliment. He can learn. I'm testing how much he's learnt.'

'We're taking Max back alive.'

'Yeah, but he's full of wrong ideas.' Jake rolled his shoulder and took a long pace towards Max with his fist raised.

'Time to beat those wrong ideas out of him.'

Gabe winced. Then he drew and aimed his gun at Jake.

'We ain't only taking Max in alive. You ain't mistreating him.'

Jake glanced from the corner of his eye and lowered his fist.

'Never thought you'd have the guts to draw a gun on me. You have, but you can holster it, and you're the first person I've given that chance to.'

'Can't do that, Jake. You're threatening an unarmed prisoner and I believe you aim to do him harm.'

Jake straightened his shoulders to stand to his full height. He chuckled and glanced at his fist.

'You're smart for a lawyer man. Didn't see you complaining about what I did to Uncas. Suppose he wasn't worth the effort.'

Gabe strode from the fire. 'Situation got out of hand with Uncas and you overreacted. I don't agree with what you did. But I understand. This situation ain't out of control.'

Max snorted. 'With Uncas the situation *was* in control. Jake knew how far he needed to push him to rile him up so he could kill him. Except no matter what Jake does, he won't rile me. I intend to live and sort him the right way.'

'You're scum, Max,' Jake muttered. 'Your sort will always cause trouble, and when you do, I'm here.'

'Those ain't our orders,' Gabe said.

'They are,' Jake snapped. 'I'm a lawman. You're a lawman. Max is scum. You're on my side, so put away your gun while you still can.'

Gabe glanced away.

Jake whirled his hand, his gun clearing leather in an instant.

In a sudden decision, Gabe fired.

Jake's gun wheeled from him to land five feet away in the dirt. Jake wrung his hand, but he was smiling.

'I didn't reckon you had the guts to fire either. Seems I was wrong about that too. And it was a good shot.' Jake flexed his fingers. 'Seen men try to do that and shoot a man's fingers clean off but you hit the gun straight on. I like men who hit what they aim at.'

Gabe's heart hammered. He gulped in relief. 'I don't want us to misunderstand each other. We *are* on the same side.'

Jake glanced at his gun. To Gabe's nod, he lifted the gun and holstered it.

As Gabe lowered his gun, Jake grabbed a branch lying beside the fire and stripped off a few twigs. Almost without Gabe realizing what he'd done, Jake leapt, rolled, and came up two yards from him. Jake swished the branch in an arc, catching Gabe's gun arm and knocking the weapon from his grip.

Gabe gripped his arm and backed a pace.

Grinning, Jake picked up the gun and handed it back to Gabe, who holstered it and flexed his arm.

'Remember.' Jake swished the branch. 'Nobody threatens me.'

'And I wasn't. We have to return Max to Carmon. We should be able to travel for two days without one of us getting riled and killing the other.'

'As you're a lawman I have no intention of killing you.' Jake widened his eyes and spat on the ground at Gabe's feet. 'But that don't stop me giving you a good whupping.'

With a great roar, Jake crashed the branch over Gabe's shoulders. Gabe fell to his knees but the branch slammed across his back, knocking him flat. In a stinging blow Jake whipped the branch across his thighs.

Gabe scrambled across the ground, trying to avoid the blows but Jake thundered them down on him. His vision darkened. An argument raged and he guessed that Max was trying to help him but blackness descended.

When he awoke, his whole body ached, but the blows had stopped. Jake's blurred shape standing over him swam into view.

'Had enough?' Jake muttered.

Gabe opened and closed his mouth but no words emerged. His vision darkened again.

'Yup,' Jake roared. 'Gabe's had enough. Time to knock sense into you now.'

'Get away!' Max shouted.

'Reckon I'll need to cut new wood for you. This branch is broken, just like you'll be.'

Gabe tried to rise but a long tunnel of darkness beckoned him.

* * *

'You fine?' Max asked.

Gabe shook himself awake.

'Suppose so,' he said, his voice croaking. He roved his hands down his body. Above the bruised feeling, no sharp pains announced themselves. He frowned as he considered his empty holster.

'He sure gave you a good whupping.'

'Yeah. Where is he?'

'He's hunting.' Max glanced around

and shivered. 'Perhaps.'

'And he trusted you to stay?' Gabe sat, wincing.

Max rubbed his bruised cheek. 'He reckons he has the measure of me.'

'He beat you too?'

'Yeah. It wasn't as bad as the one he gave you, but it was worse than the one we gave McFadden's men in the trading post.'

'Yeah, sorry I refused your offer of a drink.' Gabe licked his lips.

Max fetched a water canteen from his horse and dribbled water over Gabe's lips until Gabe grabbed the canteen and gulped a mouthful.

'I probably deserved your refusal.'

'I have no problem with you. You were just mouthing off. But Devine can't get away with killing Uncas and beating me.'

Max appraised Gabe. 'And killing my family.'

Gabe gulped a final mouthful of water and replaced the stopper.

As Max took the canteen and

returned it to his horse, Gabe rolled to his knees and stretched.

'Do you know what happened at your farm?'

Max glanced at Uncas's grave. He shrugged his jacket tighter against the dawn chill that their fire wasn't keeping at bay, then held out his hands, warming them before the fire's embers.

'Yeah, but whatever I say, no one will care.'

Gabe prodded his most tender bruises, suppressing his winces. He stood and scouted around their clearing for more dry wood. He returned and threw an armful of twigs and leaves on the fire, smothering the flames and increasing the smoke. In the sullen light, he turned to Max.

'If you die, you're right. But no matter how tough Jake acts, he won't kill me and so I'll get to explain what happened there. Can't promise that anyone will listen, but if you don't tell me . . . '

'You seem a decent man — for a

lawman.' Max glanced around their campsite, ensuring they were alone. Beyond the circle of light, the trees loomed, silent sentinels swaying in the breeze. 'I'd had some drinks so I slept them off at my pa's place, but gunfire woke me. I slipped to the door and edged it open. Devine had his gun drawn. My pa and brothers were dead.'

'Did you see him shoot them?'

Max kicked at the fire, freeing a few glowing embers.

'I could say that I did, but I can't. They were dead, and so I hightailed it out of there.'

'Were they packing guns?'

Max shrugged. 'Don't know if I heard rifle shots or a Peacemaker.'

'They're a different sound.'

'Yup, but I reckon they didn't have time to fire. Not many people aim a gun at Devine.'

'I ain't asking what you reckon,' Gabe said, keeping his voice friendly, 'just what you saw.'

Max leapt to his feet and kicked a

glowing ember. The wood flared as it rolled to a stop beyond Devine's scuffed circle and faded to oblivion.

'What I saw amounts to squat.' Max grinned without humour and leaned over the fire, the glow bathing his neck in light, creating huge shadows from his nose and cheeks. 'And nobody cares about the truth.'

'I care.' Gabe pointed at his chest.

'Don't matter.' With a snort, Max sat. 'It's still the word of one man against another. Every man has the right to meet might with might.'

'But to do that, both men must have guns. So were they packing guns?'

Max drew his legs to his chest and hugged them. He turned from Gabe and stared into the brightening sky.

'I'd like to say otherwise,' he whispered, 'but I didn't notice. That's the truth.'

'The truth will do.' Gabe rubbed his shins, finding a new sore spot. 'I visited your folk's farm. I saw the bodies. It looked like someone had put their rifles beside them.'

'Sounds likely, but you need to prove to a court what happened. It still comes down to the word of dead men against the word of a marshal.'

'But we ain't dead.'

Max snorted and shuffled closer to the fire.

'If you say so.'

★ ★ ★

Gabe awoke from his dozing as Jake stormed into their camp.

Bathed in the flat morning light, Jake threw down a clutch of birds and a rabbit and hunched over them.

Gabe shuffled from his blanket and paced to the smouldering fire. Pain announced itself along his body but he didn't rub the sore spots.

'Want food?' Jake muttered.

'You caught it?'

'Yup.'

'Then no.'

'Please yourself.' Jake kicked Max's

shin. 'And you, scum?'

'I'm with the deputy. If you caught it, I don't want it.'

'Sounds like you've had a cosy chat while I've been away. What have you decided?'

Gabe warmed his hands over the fire. 'We want nothing from you. Max ain't escaping and I ain't opposing your orders, so your job is over.'

'My job ends when Max is in Carmon's jail. Until then, I have plenty to do.'

'That ain't your job. It's to bully people into submission. As we've submitted, you've nothing more to do.'

'Seems you've talked yourself into some sense or I've explained myself. Either way I'm glad.' Jake flexed his arm. 'I'm tired of explaining.'

Gabe glanced at Max and shook his head.

When Jake had gutted his catch, he roasted the carcasses in the fire, but instead of eating them, he trussed and hung them over his saddle.

To a few orders Max kicked out the fire and they mounted their horses. As they set off the dawn glow barely lit the leaden skies.

For the first five miles Gabe hunched in his saddle, until he realized that his posture was identical to Uncas's. He sat upright. This position induced twinges from his many bruises, but he revelled in the discomfort. It let him know that he was only acting defeated.

Steady drizzle set in, the rain so fine that it resembled mist, but it dampened everything. Pearl-like droplets festooned every tree and the murk cut off their view, as if the three of them were the only people left in the world.

In their cocoon the only sounds were the steady creak of leather, the steady clop of the horses' hoofs and Jake's under-breath whistling.

Without warning, Jake stopped, halting Gabe and Max with a raised hand. He put a finger to his lips and edged into the forest, leading them. Beside a tangle of bushes he dismounted and gestured with his hands facing down. Gabe and Max dismounted and knelt.

Jake dashed back to the trail. With a branch he muddied the ground, then dashed back and led the horses into the bushes. He tethered them and knelt beside Gabe.

'What's — ' Gabe said.

Jake slammed a hand across Gabe's mouth. He swirled to Max. With the flat of his hand, he patted his holster, then lay belly down.

For an age, they lay quietly. Then the clump of horses sounded. Slipping down the trail were a file of men. Gabe counted twelve riders. Max snorted and Jake tensed, but the men continued at their steady pace.

Five minutes passed. Then Jake jumped to his feet. He slipped through the trees to the trail. With a hand to his brow, he stared along the trail, then returned.

'We can be on our way again, gentlemen,' he said.

'You reckon those men were trouble?' Gabe asked.

Jake shrugged. He turned to Max and cuffed his ear.

Gabe bunched his fists, forcing himself not to react.

Jake leaned forward. 'I'm guessing from your snort that you recognized those men.'

Max rubbed his ear. 'Tor McFadden and some of his men.'

'He have any reason to be after us?'

'Tor has plenty of reasons to want me dead.'

'Beginning to like the sound of him, but they won't get you, not when you have me to look after you.'

Jake cuffed Max again, then returned to his horse and led them back to the trail. Without further word, they continued their journey.

With the sun hidden behind thick clouds, Gabe lost all sense of direction. The trail followed the land's winding contours and although he guessed that they were heading north, he couldn't know for sure.

The day passed with no way of judging how much time passed or how many miles they covered, so that Gabe was surprised when Jake leapt from his horse and strode to a rocky outcrop.

'What you doing?' Gabe snapped.

'We won't reach Carmon before nightfall, so it's time to stop. It'll be a cold enough night. We need to start a fire early.'

Gabe glanced at the blanket of clouds that seemed to loom scant feet above his head. He jumped from his horse, slipped the blanket from his pack, and swung it round his shoulders.

Max chuckled as he swung from his horse.

'If Jake says it's time to stop, it's time to stop.'

Jake rummaged around the clearing. This high up, the sparse trees gave no protection from the chill breeze. Gabe doubted that this was the ideal place to stop, but he helped Jake collect the driest wood and before long they'd lit a smoky fire.

Jake hunkered down beside the fire. He ripped off a leg of cold rabbit and threw it to Max.

Max caught the leg and bit off a piece.

Jake grinned. 'Glad to see I've taught you sense.'

'You did squat,' Max murmured. 'Gabe did.'

Jake sliced off the other leg and threw it to Gabe.

Gabe caught the meat, but he lifted his blanket and slipped it into his pocket.

Jake considered the remaining hunk of meat and carved a slice with his thin knife.

'And how did he do that?'

Max chewed and swallowed. 'Before, I was picking my time to confront you. Now I intend to stay calm and live until we return. Then I'll explain everything I saw to Judge Daniels.'

Jake glanced at Gabe. 'Max hasn't learned the lessons he needs. What do you reckon, Sheriff Cowie's deputy?'

Sneering, Gabe paced across the clearing and stood on the outcrop. Below him, the tree line fell away sharply. The steep slope of bushes and fallen trees led down to a river that thundered by out of view.

Gabe turned to place his back to the outcrop. He glanced to the sky. The drizzle pounded into his face, chilling him to the bone and making his numerous bruises throb. He wrapped his blanket around him tighter.

'I reckon that if Judge Daniels is a fair man, he won't like what we have to tell him.'

'What's to tell him? I tried to bring in two men. One man attacked me and so I killed him. If you bring up my tapping you with a twig, it'll only prove you're the weak runt of the Cowie litter. It won't harm me.'

With a sudden flurry of anger, Gabe dashed back into the clearing, his blanket falling behind him. His back throbbed from the sudden movement, blasting away all thoughts of confrontation and he skidded to a halt.

He grabbed a branch from their pile, broke off a few twigs, and threw it on the fire. The effort produced no extra heat and Gabe slipped back inside his blanket.

Jake chuckled. 'Gabe's seeing sense. What about you, Max? Or do I need to explain more?'

Max wandered to his horse. He pulled his blanket from his pack and wrapped it around his shoulders.

'We ain't talking about you killing Uncas or your unprovoked attack on Deputy Cowie and me,' he said as he walked back, 'we're talking about you killing my family.'

'Yeah, surprised you ain't more interested in that.'

'I am. But you're trying to goad me into reacting so you can kill me and stop me talking.' Max dug his heel into the ground. He backed, marking a rough circle around the fire. On completing the circle, he stood outside it, then jumped inside. 'But no matter what you do, you won't goad me.'

'Nice circle. I'd forgotten to do that.'

'See, Jake. I saw how you pushed Uncas into acting mad and you're keeping me untied so you can try to do the same to me.'

'Reckon it'd work when a man kills someone's whole family.'

Max crossed his legs and sat, his blanket tenting around him.

'It could, but you don't know me. I'll let Daniels deal with you.'

As the rain intensified Jake looked to the sky. He let the rain run across his face, leaving channels of cleaner skin as the dust washed away.

'Daniels won't care that the worthless Randalls are no more. I went to your farm for a friendly chat and they turned on me.' Jake pulled his gun and mimed shooting at passing birds. 'I had to meet force with force.'

'That ain't true. There was a witness . . . ' Max raised his eyebrows, ' . . . and that'd be me.'

'Can't remember you being there.' Jake grinned. 'As you're alive, I guess you weren't.'

'I was and my version of what happened is different from yours.'

Gabe coughed. 'Leave this, Max. We have a long night ahead. Let's stay warm and wait until this rain clears.'

Jake ran a hand down his bushy beard, freeing a long shower of water. He lifted his hat and shook it, then pulled it low over his forehead.

'It won't ever clear for some,' he muttered.

8

As night replaced the gloom of day, the rain intensified. The spluttering fire kept some of the cold at bay — but not much.

'Can't we find a more sheltered spot?' Max muttered as he shook out his drenched blanket.

Jake grinned. 'Wondered when you'd ask. This *is* a bad location.'

'What?' Max shouted, leaping to his feet. 'You mean you stopped here because it's a bad place to camp?'

Jake chuckled. 'And it only took you two hours to figure that out.'

As Max spat on the ground, Gabe shook his head.

'Forget it, Max. We'll move to a better place. Devine can play his games in the rain.'

Jake spat into the fire. 'Max won't forget this because it's gnawing at his guts, and before too long it'll gnaw its way out. When it does, I'll be ready.'

Max smiled. 'You won't rile me enough to attack you.'

Jake reached down to the fire and pulled out a half-burnt branch. The end glowed and sizzled in the rain.

'Your attitude shows I ain't explained your role in life properly yet. If you don't want too much pain, you should change it.'

Jake swished the branch. In the gloom the end flared. A wide grin split Jake's beard. He took a long pace towards Max, who only hunched down further under his blanket.

Gabe threw his blanket down and leapt to his feet.

'I've seen enough,' he shouted. 'You ain't brutalizing our prisoner.'

Jake swung down the branch.

Max wheeled back and turned so that the flaming end crashed across his back, breaking in two. Sparks flew. He rolled, smothering the glowing embers on his back. Then he kicked and rolled from his blanket, dousing the last sparks by slapping the blanket on the ground.

While Jake picked up and discarded the largest length of broken branch, Gabe grabbed a branch from their woodpile and held it before him.

'Jake, step away from Max.'

Jake chuckled as he stared at the branch Gabe held. With deliberate slowness, he pulled his gun.

'In my experience, a man with a gun always betters a man with a stick, unless you have a clever plan in mind.'

'Whatever you're trying to do, we're still on the same side. You won't kill another lawman.'

Jake firmed his arm. 'You ain't a lawman. You're just a lawyer man.'

As the rain thundered on his hat, Gabe rubbed the brim and patted the chilled hand to his brow.

'I'm a lawyer man who happens to be Roy Cowie's son.'

'Your name don't matter to me.'

'It does. You and Roy go back a long way.'

'We do, which means I know him better than you do. I know his secrets and that includes you.' With his shoulder Jake nudged his hat to the right, shielding his eyes from the driving rain. 'He won't lose sleep if you return strung head down over your horse with a bullet in your forehead.'

Gabe stared at Jake, gauging whether he was bluffing. He slipped the branch to his left hand. Moving slowly, he lifted his hat and shook a puddle from the brim, then slipped it low over his eyes.

With his shoulders hunched, Gabe nodded towards their horses, now indistinct through the torrent of water.

'You're either prepared to kill me or you ain't, but either way, I'm ending this. Sheriff Cowie ordered me to ensure that Max returned alive, and as I believe you can't do that, I'm taking Max in — alone. Step away from him and I'll return without you. You're entitled to follow on behind and explain yourself, but you ain't coming with me.'

'Brave talk for a man with a stick.'

'And only a coward would face that man with a gun.'

'Good try, but you can't rile me.'

'Gabe's wrong,' Max said, picking up the smaller piece of the branch that Jake had broken over him. 'You're facing two men.'

Jake sneered at Max. 'You don't enter into this dispute between Gabe and me. We're fighting over you — not with you. Put that stick down or die, like the scum you are.'

Max lifted the branch higher. 'Make me.'

'No!' Gabe roared as Jake swung his gun from him. 'That's what he wants. Put it down.'

Max opened his hand, letting the branch fall, with a splash, into a muddy rivulet that ran across the clearing. To Gabe's nod, he sat.

'Now, with that sorted out,' Jake said, holstering his gun. He swirled round to Gabe and selected a firm branch. 'As I didn't beat enough sense into you before, it's time to finish the job. Just don't expect me to stop when you pass out.'

'Lay one finger on me and it'll be the last thing you do.'

'You have some courage left.' Jake advanced a pace. 'I'll soon knock that out of you.'

Gabe backed two paces, forcing Jake to step around the sizzling fire to face him, but making him stay beside the fire. Then Gabe's boot slipped in the mud.

With a lunge Jake swished the branch round. The breeze from the whipping end wafted across Gabe's face.

Gabe flinched back, then rocked forward with his weight on his right foot.

Jake lifted his hand and, as the branch rose above his head, Gabe charged him. He hit Jake full in the chest with his shoulder and pushed him back on to the fire. The fire exploded outwards, flaming branches rolling away to sizzle in the mud.

Using arms and legs, Jake thrust

Gabe back for him to land on his side. Jake rolled from the fire and kept rolling to extinguish the embers that'd stuck to his clothes. He leapt to his feet, mud and water sloughing from him. With a firm hand he batted away a smouldering lump of ash.

Jake grinned. 'Glad you did that. Got all the reasons I ever needed to beat you to a pulp.'

As Jake paced forward, Max slipped to his feet. He grabbed the branch at his feet and swung it back, preparing to club Jake over the back of the head.

Gabe kept his gaze on Jake, beckoning him onward.

Max stalked three paces and swished down the branch, but Jake turned, catching the branch as it descended and wrenching it from Max's grip.

Max stumbled and crashed to his knees in the mud.

Jake slammed his boot into Max's chin with a bone-jarring thud.

As Gabe rushed forward, Max staggered to his feet, spitting blood, and walked into Jake's large fists, which he held together and swung around, clubbing him across the cheek. Max collapsed like a fallen tree, the puddles exploding around him.

Jake turned to Gabe. 'It's just you and me now, lawyer man.'

Gabe slid to a halt and kicked at the fire. He selected an unburned branch and turned back to Jake who had selected his own branch.

As Gabe readied his stance, Jake circled him, closing with each pace. After completing a circle, Jake stood side-on and backhanded his branch.

Gabe danced back, avoiding the blow, but his foot caught in the tangle of logs by the fire and he stumbled to his knees.

In an instant Jake grabbed Gabe's branch and ripped it from his grasp to swing it into the dark. With a wide grin, he jabbed his own branch with a short-arm jab into Gabe's exposed belly.

All the air blasted from Gabe's body

as he folded over the sharp end of wood. He rolled forward, retching. With his forehead pressed into a cold puddle, he rasped in huge breaths.

With a great roar, Jake slammed his branch over Gabe's back, the wood cracking in two.

The blow flattened Gabe. He lay a moment, then staggered to his feet.

Jake was sifting through their wood pile. He stood, clutching a log, and chuckled.

'I like this one. It won't break before you do.' Jake lunged round with the thick log.

Gabe staggered back, trying to drag enough air into his lungs to stand upright. He didn't move fast enough and the log clubbed him across his temple with a solid clump.

At the last instant, Gabe had seen the log coming and rolled with the blow, but still he floundered in the mud, darkness slipping into his vision. He threw out a hand, trying to lever himself up, but the hand slipped across the wet ground and he crashed down again.

Jake loomed over him, the log held over his head as he steadied his stance, preparing to slam it down in a pulverizing blow to Gabe's head.

In desperation Gabe kicked out his right foot. The kick missed, but with a looping swirl of his leg, he caught Jake behind the knee. Gabe yanked his leg back, aiming to pull Jake over. He failed but Jake stumbled to his side as he whipped down the log, crashing it inches from Gabe's head and throwing great gouts of mud into his face.

Spitting water, Gabe rolled away, utterly drenching himself. On the second roll he staggered to his feet and walked straight into a thundering blow to the chin.

Gabe's legs became fluid as he folded. He heard a swishing noise beside him, but the cold darkness beckoned him. Then warmth joined the darkness and Gabe realized he was lying across the fire remnants. Without thinking he rolled and shook his body until the embers fell away.

He was lying in a sea of mud, sizzling branches dying around him.

Jake glared down at him, only his rain-cleaned face gleaming amidst clothes caked in thick mud and dangling from his body. He clutched another branch, which he swished back and forth.

'Got me the perfect branch now.' Jake laughed. 'The first one was too small. The other was too large. This one is just right.'

Jake lifted his hand for the first swipe.

Gabe dug his heels into the ground and pushed back, but he slipped in a deep puddle, his right hand scraping across a rock with which they'd fenced the fire. He wrapped his hand around the rock and tugged but the cloying ground held it firm.

The first blow landed across his legs. Gabe drew up his legs and folded his body over the rock. As the second blow landed across his back he closed his other hand over the rock and prised it from the ground with a huge sucking noise. With the rock free, he rolled it into his right hand.

Gabe pulled his legs up to his chest and as the next blow landed across his side, he thrust his right boot into Jake's knee.

Jake crashed on to his back. A huge blast of water sloughed away as he slid to a stop.

Gabe leapt to his feet. With dark redness exploding across his vision he stormed to Jake and lifted the rock high above his head. Even as doubt filtered into his thoughts, he crashed the rock down at Jake's head.

To protect his head Jake thrust up his left arm. The rock crunched into his arm and deflected over his head, embedding itself in the mud scant inches from his left ear.

In disgust at himself for what he'd tried to do, Gabe staggered away.

Jake sat and ran a hand along his left arm.

'You broke my arm,' he muttered.

Gabe gulped. 'You were lucky. I was aiming to kill you.'

Jake rolled to his feet and prodded his forearm, wincing.

'I could tell.'

'Let's get that fixed.' Gabe turned, his hands outstretched.

'No!' Jake roared, backing a pace. 'You ain't coming another step closer to me.'

'There's no need to carry this on.'

Jake slipped his right hand to his holster and drew his Peacemaker.

'You tried to kill a lawman. Nobody does that and lives.'

Jake lifted the gun to shoulder level and turned to the side, his right leg thrust forward, his broken arm held across his belly.

Gabe spread his feet wider. 'I'm a deputy. We're on the same side. You won't kill me.'

'Because you're a deputy you'll die with one shot. Anyone else — '

A shot rang out.

Gabe winced, but as no pain announced itself, he watched Jake collapse, his great form landing in an explosion of mud. He swirled round.

Max stood at the camp edge, a gun held outstretched but shaking.

'What? How?' Gabe babbled.

'Knew where the big man hid your gun,' Max shouted.

Gabe glanced at Jake who still lay hunched over, his forehead pressed into the mud.

'I'm obliged, but now put down the gun.'

'I can't.' Max waved his gun towards Jake. 'He's still alive.'

Jake rolled to his knees and stood. He backed a pace, his broken arm held over a dribble of blood which oozed through the thick mud caked across his chest.

'Like Gabe says, put it down,' he roared, 'or you'll suffer.'

Max firmed his gun hand. 'You ain't speaking much sense for a broken man with a bullet in him.'

Jake ruffled his soaked jacket, freeing another surge of blood from the thick mud.

'You shot a lawman. That makes two of you who'll suffer.'

'Stop!' Gabe shouted. 'We can back off from this getting worse.'

'How can this get worse?' Max shouted. 'Men who kill marshals don't live long. Every lawman in the state will search for me.'

'They won't need to. Devine ain't dead and you ain't running.'

'I'll be running for the rest of my life.'

'Which won't be for long,' Jake muttered as he backed another pace, his Peacemaker pointed down, his stance hunched.

'This doesn't need to end this way,' Gabe said, dashing across the clearing to stand between Jake and Max. 'Put down the gun, Max. Jake won't kill you if you do. He will if you don't.'

Jake chuckled as he levered himself to stand upright, but still keeping his gun pointed down.

'The lawyer man speaks sense.'

With a resigned sigh, Max held out his gun. He opened his hand.

Even as the gun plummeted to the ground, Jake hurled himself at Gabe and with a backhanded swipe of his gun hand, clubbed him down.

Max dropped to his haunches and scrambled for the gun, but Jake charged two long paces and kicked his arm away, bundling him to the ground. Max rolled to his feet and dashed to the rocky outcrop on the edge of the clearing, but then slid to a halt when faced with the sudden drop.

Jake turned his gun round and with the stock held out, he advanced on Max, aiming to pistol-whip him.

On the ground Gabe glanced around. A log was at his feet. He grabbed it and dashed after Jake. As Jake threw back his gun arm, he smashed the log into the back of Jake's legs.

Jake collapsed on the outcrop, grunting as he landed on his broken arm. He rolled over. With his back braced, he aimed his gun up at Gabe.

In desperation Gabe swung the log down, the swirling end slamming it into Jake's temple with a sickening thud.

With a pained cry, Jake rolled off the outcrop into the darkness.

Gabe staggered a pace to the edge of the outcrop. He faced the dark outlines of treetops. Below, Jake crashed through the undergrowth as he slipped down the slope.

Far below, a dull splash sounded.

Then the only sounds were the wind gusting through the trees, the rain splattering, and the river gushing below.

Gabe swirled back to Max. 'What do you reckon?'

'I reckon that if my bullet doesn't finish Devine, and you didn't break his skull, and the fall didn't get him, he's drowned.'

One careful pace at a time, Gabe edged along the rock, but a foot landed on muddy earth and slipped from under him. On his back he slithered down the slope. In a wide spread of mud and water he crashed through trees and bushes. He threw out his arms and, on the third attempt, snagged a thick bush and stopped his tumbling.

Gingerly he righted himself and picked a route down the remainder of the slope.

At the bottom the light was too faint to guide him. He peered through the thick gloom and staggered towards the gushing river, his legs encased in mud to the knees. After an age of stomping, he reached the riverside.

The swollen river surged by — the moiling water would have carried Jake off in moments.

Gabe slipped into the river. Although he couldn't get wetter, the cold dragged a gasp from his bruised body. He waded as far as he dared and rounded a tangle of gnarled trees. The river surged into the darkness. Only the occasional broken tree rolling by disturbed the dark mass.

With his teeth chattering, Gabe fought to stay upright.

'Jake!' he yelled, his voice puny against the gushing river.

When he was sure his vision wasn't improving in the darkness, he staggered back to the riverside.

Only when he started to climb the slope did the truth hit him.

'I've killed Marshal Devine.'

9

The night was as desperate and cold as any Gabe had ever faced. When he staggered to the top of the slope, neither Max nor their horses were there. Worse, the cold had permeated through to his marrow, numbing his body.

Gabe staggered to the remnants of the fire. A branch still smouldered. To protect his hand from the heat he pulled down his sleeve and grabbed the least burnt end. He dashed to a tree. In a dry spot beneath the branches, he dropped the burning wood. The wind whipped by, flaring it.

He searched for dry wood, but the rain and the dark had closed in. Everything around him was drenched. The cold and his shock at killing Devine had dulled his mind, so he staggered around, rooting through the damp undergrowth.

' 'Lo,' Max shouted. He emerged from the gloom, holding out a blanket.

With a relieved sigh, Gabe let him drape the blanket over his shoulders.

'How . . . ' Gabe's chattering teeth made more talk impossible.

Max wrapped an arm around Gabe's shoulder and shepherded him from the outcrop. They headed deeper into the forest. When they stopped they faced a sheer rock face. Trees had fallen and formed a tangle of rotting stumps, but they provided a windbreak and shelter from the rain.

Gabe rolled between two stumps where Max had lit a smoky fire. With the blanket tented over his head, he let the smoke waft into his face. His eyes watered and his breath rasped, as he flitted in and out of consciousness.

Periodically, Max nudged him awake and each time, he was warmer and his clothes were drier.

'Max,' Gabe mumbled as he started awake. He stood, letting his blanket fall.

The wind howled, flaring the fire. Beyond the tangle of trees the land was lighter. Best of all, the rain had stopped.

'Max,' he shouted. He was about to shout again but Max emerged from the forest, carrying branches.

'You fine?' Max asked.

Gabe coughed. He gulped, but judged the smoke had caused the cough.

'I am. Got to thank you for that.'

Max grinned. 'Go on. Thank me.'

'Thanks.' Gabe laughed.

Max stoked their fire. 'And I suppose I should thank you for saving me from Jake.'

'Go on. Thank me.'

'Thanks.'

'You're welcome.' Gabe edged closer to the fire. 'You reckon that he's dead?'

Max knelt beside the fire. 'Had the same worry as you. So at first light, I went down the slope and scouted around. And what we thought we heard is what happened. Jake rolled down the slope and ended up in the river. Then it carried him off.'

The fire was burning as hot as it ever had, so Gabe looped their blankets over the branches above the fire. Within seconds, steam rose.

'He might wash up somewhere.'

'Yeah, but he'll wash up drowned.' Max adjusted the blanket. 'I shot Devine, but you tumbled him into the river. Ain't clear who killed him. You tell me what our story is and I'll fit in with it.'

Gabe snorted. 'We'll tell the truth. You were right last night. When someone kills a marshal, every lawman in the state will search for the culprit. Trying to hide what happened will cause problems, so we start with the truth and nobody can shake us from it.'

'Sometimes the truth needs encouragement.'

Gabe sat on a stump. Although he was dry and warm, he held out his hands to the fire. His guts rumbled. Then he remembered last night's foresight. He fished in his pocket for the rabbit meat. It was grey, cold, and coated in dirt, but Gabe ripped it in two and held out a piece.

'Lying might work for a while, but what happens when Devine washes up with a bullet in his guts?'

Max took the meat and took a large bite. 'I once saw a body that had been in the water — ain't much of a sight for anyone. Guessing as nobody could know how such a person died.'

Gabe rubbed away the worst of the dirt from the meat and took a gritty bite.

'Perhaps, but the river winds down to Monotony. If someone finds him, it'll be soon. We can't hide this. We tell the truth about what happened last night — and at your family's farm — and there'll be no problems. Devine was a violent man. Everyone will know that.' Gabe wolfed the last lump of meat. 'The truth will fit the facts.'

Gabe scraped the dried mud from his clothes and completed his drying process. Having spent time cold, it was with reluctance that he dragged himself from the fire and headed back to the trail.

They released Jake's horse and led their own horses to the drying trail. For the first time the sun broke through and Gabe lifted his chin to the warmth.

Max mounted his horse. 'Devine didn't know why he had to take me in and I reckon you don't know either.'

Gabe rolled into the saddle and turned his horse to the trail.

'The reason ain't important. I have my duty, and I'm taking you in, but I'll deal with you fairly.'

'You ain't taking me in.' Max removed his hat and considered it. 'I'm taking myself in.'

'Glad to hear it. What changed your mind?'

'Nothing. I was always taking myself in.'

'When we caught you, you were running south. That's a mighty odd way of taking yourself in.'

Max paced his horse to the edge of

the rocky outcrop. The clouds had lifted, providing a panoramic view of the river snaking east through the forest and their trail winding north and south. As Gabe joined Max on the outcrop, Max lifted his hand to his brow, shielding his eyes from the sun.

'This must be the highest spot around here. Carmon is over there.' Max pointed. In the distance, a lighter slash of green marked the onset of cleared farmland. 'Wouldn't have minded seeing my home town for the last time. You see. I ain't taking myself in to Carmon.'

'Why?' Gabe asked.

'I'll go to any place where I can get justice, but I'll never get it in Carmon.'

'From what I hear, Roy Cowie has forged a decent law-abiding town. If you can't get justice there, you'll get it nowhere.'

'I don't agree,' Max whispered. 'Not when the justice you is seeking is against Roy Cowie.'

'What?' Gabe snapped, turning his

159

horse round to draw alongside Max.

Max stared at the southern trail. 'You heard right. I've done nothing wrong, or at least nothing that it's worth getting the roughest lawman in the West to track me down for.'

'Then why is everyone after you?'

Max turned to Gabe, but his eyes were downcast.

'I know how Roy Cowie and Tor McFadden got rich,' he muttered, then sighed as if stating that fact was a relief. 'Except when I decided to discover if anyone was interested, I found my life would be short. So I headed for Waltersville. Uncas said I might find someone who ain't in their pay to listen to me there.'

'And you still reckon you have that chance?'

'Yup. But if we head north, I'll never get it.' Max met Gabe's gaze.

'You're in my keep,' Gabe said, using his calmest voice. 'You'll be safe. Whatever you want to say about whomever, you'll get that chance.'

Max narrowed his eyes. 'Even if it's against your pa?'

Gabe threw up his hands and snorted. 'Don't know him. I've spent more time with Devine. Don't matter to me if you have a problem with him.'

'I believe you. But practically everyone in Carmon works for Roy Cowie or Tor McFadden.' With a steady hand, Max scratched his bristled chin. 'I reckon I'll have plenty of guns aiming my way if I return.'

Gabe glanced back and forth along the trail. 'All right. I've never run from trouble before, but sometimes you have to be sensible. Let's hope we get to Waltersville before Devine washes up and we're the State's most wanted men.'

At a steady pace, they rode down the trail. The rain had washed away their markings from their previous passage. When they were through the first clump of trees, the south opened up, giving them a clear view for miles ahead.

Gabe narrowed his eyes. Further down the slope a rising dust cloud surrounded a group of riders.

'They're the first people we've seen since McFadden's men yesterday.'

He turned to Max, who already peered at the dust.

'Yeah,' Max muttered. 'And we shouldn't wait to discover where they're going.'

Max pulled on his reins and headed back northward. Gabe trotted after him, picking the best route on the slippery trail.

'You reckon that they're after you?' he shouted, drawing alongside.

'I'm taking Devine's advice and not waiting to find out.'

Gabe glanced over his shoulder. The riders were still a mile away, but near enough to count six men.

'They might not be McFadden's men.'

When they reached the top of the slope, Max spurred his horse for more speed.

'Don't matter,' he shouted over his shoulder. 'Everyone is after me.'

As they speeded to a gallop, Gabe realized that after all their discussion they were heading to Carmon.

* * *

Sheriff Frank Cowie glanced up as Deputy Wiles wandered into his office.

'What's wrong?' Frank asked.

Wiles pushed back his hat. 'Got news. Some folks saw Devine and two other men riding south beyond Monotony and another man riding ahead who was probably Max. Devine was gaining on him.'

'That ain't news. Devine failing to get his quarry is news.'

'Got more though. Young cowhand found a saddled horse roaming by the woods south of Monotony. He scouted around and found a body.'

'What did Sheriff Yates say?'

'He sent the body to us. Said we might be more interested. We are.'

Wiles beckoned and Frank followed him outside. A horse stood by the rail outside with a body strung across the back. A crowd had gathered, staring at the body with the usual mixture of distaste and interest.

Frank balked at the body's rank odour. 'Wiles, show him some dignity. Cover him up.'

'Sorry, boss, but look at the body first.'

Frank paced to the body. Gunshots peppered its back. He lifted the ginger-haired head.

'See what you mean.' Frank let the head fall back. Without further word, he strode to his cart.

While Wiles directed the townsfolk away, he manoeuvred the cart to the horse. Then they swung the body on to the cart.

Frank covered the body, then headed out of town and back to the Cowie ranch.

At the ranch, a familiar horse was outside. Frank didn't expect it, but somehow its presence fitted in. He jumped from his cart. With a quick gesture, he lit a match on his boot and puffed on a cheroot.

He'd almost finished his smoke when Billy McFadden emerged from the ranch dressed in work clothes.

Frank ground out the cheroot under his boot and strode from his cart.

'Afternoon, Billy,' he said. 'You've missed Thelma. She's in town.'

'Is she?' Billy glanced away. 'Yeah, I knew. I came to see your father on business.'

'Thelma said you'd be away for a while.'

'I was. But I'm back.'

'Say hello to her for me if you see her in town.'

'I ain't heading that way. I'm in a hurry.'

Billy lifted a foot to mount his horse, but Frank slammed a hand on his shoulder. Billy flinched.

'Don't go yet. Got something you ought to see.'

Billy frowned and turned. 'Make it quick.'

Frank sauntered to his cart. When Billy joined him, he swung back the thick cloth on the back.

The body lay flat on its back, its sunken eyes staring upward.

Billy shrugged. 'This looks like your problem.'

'It is, except this man works for Tor.'

Billy grabbed the cloth and covered the body. 'If you want more details, take him to Pa. He'll know his name.'

'Don't need to. This is Walt Perkins.' Frank considered Billy's blank expression. 'I'm surprised you didn't recognize him. He's ridden with you plenty of times.'

Billy turned from the cart and strode back to his horse.

'Plenty of people have ridden with me plenty of times. I don't know all their names.'

Frank paced after him. 'Fine. I'll see Tor. See if he has more interest in this than you do.'

Billy lifted a foot, then lowered it again. 'I can save you a journey. Pa ain't at the ranch.'

'How do you know that? You're in a hurry and you ain't got time to see Thelma except you know Tor's whereabouts.'

'What you getting at?' Billy snapped, placing his hands on his hips. 'I had nothing to do with Walt's death. If you want I can get men to — '

'I ain't accusing you.' Frank tipped back his hat and glanced away. 'Sorry. This is my first murder. Guess I'm flustered.'

Billy patted Frank's shoulder. 'I'm sure you'll deal with it.'

'Yeah, and Thelma's been missing you. Then you not going to see her irritated me.'

'Understood. We'll be family soon. I'd hate us to have any misunderstandings. If I can go, I'll swing by Carmon and see her.'

'You do that.'

Billy mounted his horse and rode

from the ranch. Once outside, he headed west, away from Carmon.

Frank strode into the ranch house. He paused in the hall, ordering his thoughts, then wandered to the living-room. Roy looked up.

'It's early, boy. Hope you ain't trusting Deputy Wiles with looking after my town or I won't have a town left.'

Frank forced a chuckle. 'I've returned for advice.'

'I'm always happy to provide that.' Roy raised his eyebrows. 'Even when you don't want it.'

Frank laughed, unforced. 'This time it's wanted. Walt Perkins is outside.'

'Walt's one of Tor's men. What does he want with us?'

'He doesn't want anything now. Someone killed him on the trail beyond Monotony.'

Roy glanced through the window, a small smile on his lips.

'Billy will have a say in what you should do, but he's heading back to his ranch.'

'I spoke with him. He said it was my concern.' Frank took a pace towards Roy, studying his smile. 'I ain't had anybody die on my patch. Then Devine arrives and before long, the bodies pile up. Even Deputy Wiles could spot a connection.'

Roy grinned wider than Frank had seen for many a year.

'You're probably right.'

Frank scratched his head and paced from side to side, patting his fist into his hand as he made each of his points.

'Most of the Randalls are dead. Max is alive, but he probably won't see this winter. They're people with whom we don't get along. Now Walt Perkins is dead.'

'Walt's with Tor.' Roy gritted his teeth. 'We get on fine with him.'

Frank stopped his pacing and lifted a finger. 'Same problem. They're people we're close to, either in hatred or in business. Maybe you want to help me complete the connections.'

Roy pursed his lips and considered

Frank. 'I can't. You're the lawman. The sooner you know that, the sooner you'll figure it out.'

Frank narrowed his eyes. 'Does that mean you know what the connection is, but you won't tell me?'

Roy turned to stare through the window. 'I didn't say that, but either way, this is still your problem.'

'As people keep telling me.' With a slow shake of his head, Frank stalked to the door. 'Just reckoned you might like a say before I investigate the problem.'

'Why?' Roy whispered, the word barely audible.

Frank paused at the door, staring into the hall. 'In case you don't like the answers I find.'

Without waiting for a reply, Frank strode into the hall and from the ranch.

* * *

As Gabe and Max crested the next hill, Gabe glanced back at the following riders. For over an hour they'd suffered

170

this pursuit and although their horses were tiring and they were slowing with each passing mile, their pursuers weren't gaining on them.

Gabe drew his horse closer to Max.

'What you reckon?' he shouted.

Max glanced back. 'About them not trying to catch us?'

'Yeah.'

'The same as you. They don't need to run us down when we're heading in the direction they want us to go.'

Gabe glanced from the trail at the thick wall of trees flanking them.

'Are there any other trails beside this one?'

'We'll cross the trail to Monotony soon, but that's only five miles out of Carmon; excepting that, I don't know any.'

'Then we'll make our own trail.'

'I'm with you,' Max hollered. 'Just give the word.'

'Slow, and give the horses a breather. After the next ridge, we head for cover.'

Max pulled back on the reins. The

riders behind slowed too.

Max and Gabe crested the slope. Gabe counted to ten, then glanced back. Their pursuers were out of sight.

'Go left,' he shouted.

They swung from the trail and headed towards the forest, galloping hard down the hillside. The forest closed fast, the trees an impenetrable wall. Gabe glared ahead, searching for the gap that had to be there.

They were twenty yards away when the slimmest of gaps in the mass of trees opened. Gabe pointed and headed for it, slowing as late as possible. He ducked, branches whipping across his face as they hurtled through the gap. Then they were in the forest.

Their horses reared and whinnied. The route ahead was so thicketed that Gabe saw no way through.

Gabe glanced over his shoulder, where the men crested the hill and skidded to a halt as they hollered to each other and searched for where they'd gone.

With his horse balking at picking a route through the dense undergrowth, Gabe leapt down. Max did the same and they led their horses onward, thrashing branches aside as they fought into the undergrowth.

They walked thirty yards. Gabe glanced back, but the trees had closed his view beyond the forest.

As another branch scratched across his face, Gabe stopped and searched for a better route.

'What you reckon, Max?'

'We're clearing a trail even I could follow. We might make better speed on foot.'

Gabe fought a losing battle with another thick branch, then turned to Max, shaking his head.

'Nope. The trail we'd make would still be too obvious.'

'What we going to do then?'

Gabe pointed to a clump of fallen trees. 'Fight.'

To Max's nod Gabe passed his reins to him. Max led the horses twenty yards further on and tethered them to a branch.

Gabe knelt behind the fallen trees, his gun resting on the topmost log. Max returned and matched his posture.

Gabe listened for the obvious noises anyone would make in crashing through the thick tangle of undergrowth. But except for the occasional hollering in the distance, Gabe only heard the trees rustling.

Fifteen minutes passed before a crunch sounded and someone cursed.

Gabe nodded to Max and slipped behind the log. He listened to the occasional curse, the sounds closing. Gabe nudged Max and held up two fingers, then shuffled further down.

Through the undergrowth, two men approached, guns held out as they edged forward.

Gabe lined his sights. With an elbow he nudged Max.

'Five more paces,' he mouthed.

The two men closed, wasting their energy on struggling through the bushes and branches and not guarding against an ambush.

On five, Gabe tightened his finger on the trigger.

Max fired, Gabe firing a second later.

Both men fell, disappearing from view in the thick undergrowth.

'Got 'em,' Max muttered and started to rise.

Gabe pushed Max down. 'Ain't sure. I reckon the one on the left dived.'

Max smiled. 'That'd be your one.'

'It would,' Gabe muttered.

A gunshot whistled a foot over Gabe's head. Gabe hit the ground and rolled on to his belly. He glanced over the log. He only saw trees.

'We'll have to flush him out,' Max said. 'Or more to the point, you'll have to flush him out.'

Gabe nodded. 'Cover me.'

Max swung round and rested his gun on the log.

Gabe vaulted the log. As Max fired another round of gunfire, he dashed into the undergrowth to the man's right. On the fifth shot, Gabe dived behind a thick bush.

Flat on his belly and using his elbows, Gabe edged forward. He pushed through the bush and on slipping enough of the tangled branches aside he had a clear view.

Ten yards ahead, a man lay sprawled beside a tree. He was still.

More gunfire sounded to Gabe's left. Gabe leapt to his feet.

The other man was dashing to Max's position. He leapt behind a tree stump, swung his gun on top, and fired at Max from only five yards away.

Gabe pushed from the bush, the leaves and branches snagging on his clothing and tumbling him out.

The man flinched and fired at Gabe as he emerged. With no protection Gabe gritted his teeth and fired.

On the second shot, the man spun and fell, landing on his back.

Within seconds, Max had vaulted the log and stood over the man, kicking away his gun. He knelt by the man and fingered his neck. He nodded.

With his shoulders hunched, Gabe trudged back to their log. When Max returned, he was smiling.

'That's two down and four to go,' Max said. 'And if two couldn't get us out, four won't.'

For the next thirty minutes, Gabe expected another attack to follow. Every rustle of leaves, every bird chirping caused his heart to hammer and his palms to sweat.

'Hot damn,' Gabe muttered. 'How much longer before they come?'

'Patience. This could go on all day and night.'

'I thought I *was* patient. We should see what they're doing.'

Max nodded and they edged through the forest back along their obvious route. When they reached the tree line, they crawled forward and peered down to the trail.

Below, the four riders on the trail stared in their direction.

'They're settling in, waiting for us to

make our move.' Max smiled. 'If they're planning on waiting, I reckon we should head through the forest. We could get some distance.'

Gabe glanced back into the forest, imagining clawing past endless trees. He gulped.

'No. We wait.'

For the next hour, they watched the riders talk amongst themselves. Just as the wait was eroding Gabe's nerves again, the riders spread out and faced the southward trail.

A new line of riders galloped over the hilltop and slowed to a halt.

'There's another ten men there,' Max said.

'Twelve.' Gabe narrowed his eyes. 'No, fourteen.'

10

Searing pain dragged Jake Devine into consciousness. He shook himself, disorientated. With questing fingers, he confirmed that he'd lost his gun, but he still had both his knives.

With his right arm he pushed up. Thick mud and water sucked him down.

With water sloshing around him, Jake rolled on to his back. He'd washed into a tangle of trees at the side of a milling river.

Jake shivered and stood, water cascading from him. With his shoulders hunched he sloshed to the riverbank and rolled on to dry land. He counted his numerous injuries. The most insistent pain came from his left arm. He ran his right hand down his forearm. A grating pain announced itself.

He blinked twice, but his vision

remained blurred. He rolled to his knees and another stab of pain from his chest told him that the bullet wound gave him more to worry about than his broken arm.

While he breathed steadily, the shivering started.

Jake gritted his teeth, trying to stop the shaking, but he failed.

He rolled to his feet, his broken arm held across his chest, cradling his two biggest sources of pain in the same place, and staggered from the river. He was deep in the forest, roots and thick tangles of fallen branches around him.

With slow paces he staggered to higher ground away from the boggier land around the river and slumped beside a fallen tree.

He collected dead branches, moss and brittle leaves and piled them beside the tree. For the next ten minutes he made a fire.

Using one hand, the fire took longer to start and when the first fragile flames emerged, the cold had chilled Jake to the marrow. He hung over every spark, every puff of smoke, letting their warmth fill him.

Lost in time, Jake's life condensed to the flames and the wood he fed the fire. When the fire had built its momentum, he collected enough spare kindling and forced the quickest burning fire he could. He stripped off and laid his clothes over the tree behind the fire. He hunkered down, trying to stop the shivering, using just willpower. He couldn't at first, but by degrees the heat permeated his body.

When the shivering stopped, he prodded his arm and confirmed that it was straight and his fingers still moved. As one problem solved itself, Jake smiled. He'd had to pull bones back into place once before, but he'd been younger and stronger then.

He cut four branches, stripped off their leaves and twigs. With slices of bark to secure them, he encased his arm. The makeshift splint would keep the arm from suffering more damage while it knitted, provided he protected it.

He examined his chest. The bullet hole was below his first rib. From the ragged raised skin around the wound only a dribble of blood seeped out.

Jake thanked his luck again that the bullet hadn't ripped through anything more serious. He threw more kindling on the fire, getting it as hot as he could. When the fire was so hot that he couldn't stare at it, he fished in his boot for his thin knife and leaned back against the tree.

Ideally, he needed to slip a probe or forceps under the bullet and lever it out. With neither of these, he would have to improvise.

With the aid of a stone, he bent the end of his thin knife to the side. Then he heated both his knives. When they cooled, he grabbed a branch and bit hard into it, pulling it back so his mouth was in a wide smile.

With more branches piled at his side, he laid his broken arm across his chest.

He placed his fingers around the bullet hole and pulled the skin taut, then slipped the larger knife into the hole.

As he had tensed himself, he had ignored the pain. Then, with a surge, something tore. He glanced down as fresh, bright blood welled around the cut. As he delved deeper, he bit into the branch, but the knife scraped across something. The sound was dull, and so it wasn't bone. Jake scraped the knife to the side. He bit into his branch as the knife slipped from the bullet and tore through muscle.

He spat out the broken branch and edged his broken arm to a new, thicker branch. With that in his mouth, he slipped the knife further in, measuring the distance into his chest. When he felt he'd cut enough, he slipped the knife out.

He slipped the thin knife into his wound. He moved as slowly as possible, edging it through his torn flesh past the bullet — if he hadn't cut enough he could push the bullet even further in.

When he judged he'd gone far enough in, he wriggled the knife to the side. In the tight wound, he needed to slip it under the slug and lever it out. He pulled.

The knife tagged on his raw wound, dragging through the ripped layers of muscles and skin. Jake bit deep into the branch and pulled again.

Darkness filled his vision.

When light returned he spat the broken branch from his mouth, glanced down, but only saw blood. He wiped his chest and pressed on either side of the wound, but saw only ragged flesh when it popped open.

Jake swore a silent oath for being too timid the first time. Then, with more determined strokes, he bent the thin knife to a greater angle. He warmed the knife, then slipped it into the wound. The knife scraped the bullet. He turned the knife away and sliced it through muscle, then turned it back, slipping the bent end under the bullet.

He pulled up and glared down. A

misshapen slug lay on his belly.

He pocketed the slug, then strapped his larger knife to a branch, producing a spear, and laid it in the fire. He had met doctors who said you should keep a wound open to encourage the green pus, but Jake didn't believe them.

When the bindings smouldered and the knife glowed, Jake counted to five. Then he pulled the spear from the fire and laid the glowing knife on his chest.

Darkness stole him.

He awoke seconds or minutes later. He prised the cooling knife from his wound, the sharp smell of cooked meat greeting him. Then he cut his shirt into strips and bound his chest tightly, using the remaining strips for a sling.

He kicked out the fire and headed north, making steady progress through the forest. With his arm and chest throbbing with an insistent rhythm, he walked tall as he pushed as many branches away as possible.

Forest stretched before him with nothing but animal trails, so he kept the river to his right.

When the sun edged towards the tree line, Jake's stomach grumbled. With a knife, he could hunt, but as he needed to keep travelling, he couldn't eat anything fulfilling.

Berries and roots provided some nourishment. Then he resumed walking.

As the light dropped a fire to his left illuminated the trees, and the inviting smell of cooking drifted to him.

Grinning as his luck held again today, he headed for the fire. Two men sat around it, roasting a hare on a spit.

To avoid surprising them, Jake crunched twigs and rustled leaves.

When the men grabbed their rifles, Jake coughed.

'I ain't trouble,' he hollered. 'Just a traveller like you, looking for warmth and perhaps a chance to share food.'

'Come out so we can see you, friend,' the first man shouted.

'I'm here.' With a hand raised Jake

staggered into the clearing.

'You ain't had much luck.' The first man lowered his rifle.

The second man leaned to the first man and whispered something. They both turned back to Jake. Slow smiles spread.

'Now look what's here.' The second man aimed his rifle at Jake. 'We have ourselves a marshal.'

Jake narrowed his eyes. 'And?'

'Have you ever met Walt Perkins?'

'Not that I know of.'

The man grinned. 'This is Mort Falcon and I'm Carl Perkins. I'm Walt's brother.'

★ ★ ★

Gabe and Max watched the men on the trail.

For an hour, the men just talked. Just as Gabe feared that they were waiting for even more men to arrive and flush them out, two men leapt on their horses and galloped north. Two other men leapt on their horses and headed south.

'The way I see it,' Max leaned to Gabe, 'they're either aiming to outflank us or they're fetching more men.'

'You'd reckon they had enough. There are only two of us.'

'Perhaps Devine has washed up and they figure that the men who killed him ain't to be toyed with.'

Gabe chuckled and awaited developments.

Five minutes later, two more men mounted their horses and headed north. Two others headed south. The remaining men stood in a group gesticulating in various directions before two others rode south, leaving six men watching the forest.

'How many reinforcements do they reckon they need?'

Max counted on his fingers and nodded.

'I know what they're doing, and fetching reinforcements would be better.' Max rolled on to his side and grabbed a twig. He drew lines in the dirt and placed a cross beside a line. 'We're here, and these are the main trails. They're covering them all. They've sent men to guard the trails to Monotony, Beaver Ridge — even the westward trail. We're doomed.'

Gabe rubbed his chin, then pointed at the crosses Max had placed over each trail.

'Then we should do the one thing they don't expect us to do.' With a lunge, Gabe grabbed a twig and drew a large cross across one of the lines on Max's diagram. 'We head for Carmon.'

'That's suicide.'

Gabe threw the twig over his shoulder. 'According to you, every route we take leads to death. So we take the one they won't expect.'

Max rolled back on his front to stare down at the trail.

'I like your logic, but it won't work. Every man in Carmon will be against us. We need another option.'

They stared at the men below. Then Gabe lowered his head.

'I ain't asked as you don't want to answer, but you have to tell me now. Why exactly do so many people want you dead? What do you know about how Roy Cowie and Tor McFadden got rich?'

'If it ain't changing your actions, I don't have to tell you.'

'Knowing might tell me what we're facing. And when a man knows what he faces, he has a chance.'

Max stared back. Then his shoulders slumped.

'Thirty years ago, three men travelled west. They decided this was a good place for a town. They were right. They were Tor McFadden, Roy Cowie and Seth Randall. Now Tor heads the richest family in town, Roy heads the second and Seth . . . ' Max sighed. 'The Randalls are dead and nobody was sad to see us go.'

'Not everyone prospers. Being bitter is a poor reason.'

Max pointed down the hill. 'Tor McFadden is on the left. Will Sidings, his ranch boss, is beside him. Why would key workers on Carmon's richest ranch look for a drunk who talks too much in saloons?'

'You tell me.'

'Because I . . . ' With his twig Max scratched a line, then hurled it away. 'Roy and Tor skim profits from the trade that passes through Carmon.'

'You got proof?'

'I only have rumours.'

Gabe narrowed his eyes, then smiled. 'Are you saying that you've avoided answering my questions because you know squat?'

'That sums it up.' Max laughed. 'I know squat.'

Gabe chuckled, the chuckle growing. He clamped a hand over his mouth and glanced down the slope.

'So why is everybody after you if you know squat?'

'I know squat but they don't know I know squat.'

Gabe coughed and cleared his throat, forcing down a laugh.

'Why do they reckon you know something?'

'Because I shot my mouth off. Pa always said it'd get me into trouble, and he was right.'

'So if we get you somewhere safe and you testify, what you'll say won't do anything?'

Max stared at the ground. 'Nope. Might get me jailed for being malicious — if that's a crime — but beyond that, I can't prove anything.'

'So all that talk of testifying in Waltersville was just talk?'

Max lowered his hat over his eyes. 'Sorry, Gabe, but people are right about me. I'm all kinds of bad. Everything I've told you is lies — even about me hearing Devine shooting my family. I wasn't there.'

'Except you've told me one truth.' With his head on one side, Gabe stared at Max until he looked up. 'You know squat.'

Doubled over, he backtracked into the forest, Max following. Fifty yards in, Gabe stood and stretched his back.

'You have a plan?' Max asked, joining him.

'Yup. It's time you returned to Carmon and let everyone know the truth.'

'But I know squat,' Max snapped. 'I told you.'

Gabe smiled. 'I know.'

11

With his hands tied behind his back Jake Devine sat against a rock, his legs drawn to his chest.

'What you waiting for?' Jake muttered.

Carl glanced up from the fire, his cheekbones prominent in the flickering light.

'We're waiting for someone. Don't reckon he'll be pleased if we kill you before he gets here.' Carl spat into the fire. 'He hates snooping lawmen.'

Jake flexed his shoulders and ran his feet forward so that less of his weight was on his arms.

'Do you know which lawman I am?'

'There ain't many men who don't know Marshal Jake T. Devine.' Carl grinned. 'And what does the T stand for?'

Jake flexed his right arm, but the

bonds were secure.

'Untie me and I'll tell you.'

'Don't see that happening.'

Jake flexed his left arm instead. The rope didn't give but the movement sent a stab of pain grating down his broken arm. He winced and glared at Carl.

'Any chance of food?'

'Nope.'

'A blanket?'

'Nope. And I ain't falling for those tricks. We ain't getting close to you so you can try something. You ain't getting anything until later. Then you won't like what you get.'

'Follow orders then, scum.' Jake sat as straight as possible. 'I wanted to keep this civilized for when I bring you in later.'

With a chuckle, echoed by Mort, Carl poked at the fire.

'You won't be bringing us in later.'

'I will. Then I'll have to consider whether you've mistreated a lawman. If you have, you'll swing. If you've been co-operative, things might be different.' Jake spat to the side. 'Then you'll get a last meal before you swing.'

Carl turned from Jake, but Mort snorted.

'You ain't riling us, Marshal,' he said.

'Sure won't. You ain't bright enough to rile.'

Mort swaggered to Jake and loomed over him.

'Do you know how the Shawnee treat their prisoners?' Mort pulled Jake's knives from his boot. He tapped them against each other, then returned the thin knife to his boot and gestured with the larger one. 'Guess I have enough time to show you.'

Jake glared at the knife. 'I'd like to see you try. Scum like you don't frighten me.'

Mort turned the knife and felt the edge with his thumb.

'You have a strange way of trying to rile me.' He raised his eyebrows. 'Ain't working.'

Carl wandered across the clearing to

stand beside Mort. He slapped his shoulder.

'Take no chances. He's devious. Ignore him and stay back.'

Mort nodded. 'Yeah. We'll wait.'

Jake chuckled. 'I can see who's the boss between you two. You like working for Carl?'

As Carl turned, Mort half-turned, then turned back. 'I don't work for Carl,' he muttered.

'You took his orders. You work for him.'

With a dismissive gesture Mort waved and backed a pace.

'You don't know.'

Jake roared his laughter. 'Oh. It's like that, is it? Never have guessed it, but there it is.'

Carl wandered back to the fire, but Mort placed his hands on his hips.

'What's like what?'

'Ain't saying anything. Men can get awful lonely on the trail. I understand. Not interested myself, but I understand.'

Mort narrowed his eyes. 'What in tarnation are you blathering on about?'

Jake shrugged, suppressing a wince as his broken arm snagged.

'Just saying that I understand why you take Carl's orders.'

'Let's hear it,' Mort muttered.

'Like I say, a man can get lonely on the trail. In certain saloons there are ladies who can help a man out. But that ain't to every man's taste.' Jake licked his lips. 'That's where you come in. You're a man who likes following orders. Reckon you can be most obliging.'

The colour rose on Mort's face. With a great roar, he charged across the camp and slammed his boot into Jake's thigh.

Jake roared his laughter louder.

With his face bright red, Mort reached down to grab the bindings on Jake's chest, but with a short nudge, Jake slammed his forehead into Mort's nose. A great explosion of redness showered away.

Mort stumbled, throwing his hands to his face and Jake kicked his legs to the side, tumbling him down. In a second, Jake was on him. He had kept sight of his knife through his baiting and he closed his right hand on it.

From the corner of his eye, he saw Carl leap to his feet and draw his gun.

With a great swipe of his hand behind his back, Jake sliced through the bonds. Dampness gushed over his hands as he sliced through his own flesh in his eagerness to be free. Then he was on his feet and underhanding the knife.

Carl dived, the knife swirling by him.

Having distracted Carl, Jake kicked Mort over and scrabbled for his gun. A gunshot plumed inches from his hand, but Jake closed his hand on the weapon and in a smooth motion aimed it towards Carl. With his first shot he blasted him through the chest. As Carl collapsed, Jake rolled to his feet. Then he fired another two bullets into Carl's guts.

Jake aimed his gun back to the prone

Mort, but he was unconscious.

Jake flexed his back and checked that his arm was still straight. He ran his fingers along the bandages around his chest and wasn't surprised to find a damp stain above the bullet wound. He rummaged through Mort's and Carl's belongings, finding a bottle of whiskey. He unbound his wound and doused it, wincing at the stinging pain, then gulped a good swig. For bandages he shredded Carl's shirt, wrapping the slicing cut on his arm too.

As he finished, Mort stirred.

Jake wandered across the camp and kicked Mort awake. He grinned and pulled the knife from his boot.

'Now,' he muttered, 'what was you telling me about how the Shawnee treat their prisoners?'

★　★　★

Gabe and Max abandoned their horses and on foot trudged northward through the undergrowth. They were on the wrong side of the trail to Carmon, so they stayed close enough to the forest edge to judge when they could cross the trail, but far enough in that McFadden's men wouldn't hear their progress.

Their journey was slow. The tangle of undergrowth caught their feet, making every pace a battle. After thirty minutes they fought to the forest edge and peered back. To their delight, they'd traversed a bend in the trail and McFadden's men were out of sight.

They slipped from the trees and across the trail. But as they faced another dense thicket of trees they turned north and walked beside the forest instead.

They took turns staring back and forth as they now made proper progress. Throughout the afternoon they twice had to slip into the trees when riders approached, and such was the closeness of the trees that they disappeared within seconds. Both times the riders didn't slow and when they'd passed, Gabe and Max headed onward.

To avoid two of McFadden's men, who guarded the trail to Monotony, they needed a detour back into the forest, but at sunset, from the crest of a hill, they looked down at Carmon.

As the sky darkened, they dashed across the fields, heading for the church, the largest landmark in town. When they reached the back of the church, Gabe leaned against the wall and patted Max's back.

'That was a long journey,' he said. 'You ready for the next bit?'

'As I'll ever be.'

They slipped round the side of church and on to the main road. People milled about as they finished their business before night enveloped the town.

Gabe walked straight into the road, but Max sidled from the church and edged along the boardwalk. He kept his back to the wall while walking sideways.

'Don't walk like that,' Gabe murmured.

Max stopped and glanced around.

'Don't want anyone to see me.'

Despite the situation, Gabe smiled. 'Walking like *that* will make sure people see you.'

Max joined Gabe. He pulled his hat low and maintained a brisk pace down the road.

To avoid catching anyone's eye Gabe mumbled animated conversation to Max, until he reached the sheriff's office, where he walked straight in.

'Howdy, Frank,' he said as he threw back the door.

Frank clattered his feet from his desk. With his mouth wide open he stared at Gabe, then smiled.

'Sure am glad to see you.'

Gabe edged to the side to let Max pass him. 'Got someone with me.'

'Max, I'm not so glad to see you.' Frank glanced over Gabe's shoulder. 'Where's Devine?'

Gabe glanced back at Max, who looked away. 'Devine's whereabouts is a long story.'

'As you once said to me, I have time

for the short version.'

Gabe drew in a long breath. 'Sorry. That'll have to wait. You'll have to trust me.'

Gabe locked the door and glanced through the window, but none of the passing people looked at the office.

Frank joined Gabe by the window. He stared outside a moment.

'Still obliged that you brought in Max.' He turned to Max. 'And so *you* are under arrest.'

'Gabe didn't bring me in,' Max snapped. 'I've brought myself in.'

Frank folded his arms and cocked his head to one side.

'That's mighty noble of you. Sure it'll help you when Judge Daniels arrives.'

Max snorted. 'You don't get this, do you? You ain't arresting me because you have no charges against me. I'm here for my own protection. Gabe has convinced me that you'll do that and I believe him.'

Frank glanced at Gabe, then stalked to his desk and grabbed his keys. He unlocked the door at the back of his office. With an oil-lamp held aloft against the blackness beyond the cell door, he led the two men down a corridor that snaked to the left.

Gabe traced the route and realized that they were under the court. The row of cells had no view of the outside world. The back walls were solid and at the front the cell bars faced the corridor.

Frank opened the end cell, the door squeaking. He beckoned Max inside.

With a glance at Gabe, Max strode inside.

Frank put the oil-lamp inside the cell and closed the door. He held the door, then opened it again.

'Never had a non-prisoner in these cells. So I suppose it's up to you if you want the door closed.'

Max swung the cell door open, then closed it. 'I'll accept closed but not locked.'

'I'll look in on you later with food.'

'Obliged.'

Frank nodded to Gabe and paced down the corridor and outside.

Max gripped the bars. 'I'll be fine in here, Gabe. I have plenty of thinking to do.'

Gabe shook his head. 'Thinking is the last thing you need. Tell the truth. It can't harm the innocent but it sure can harm the guilty. Do it like we said.'

Max turned and strode the three paces to the back wall where he flopped on the bed. He provided the barest of nods.

Gabe left him. In the main office, he swung the door to the cells shut, but didn't lock it.

'You seem to be friendly with Max,' Frank said while staring through his window.

'Yup. We've been through some things and that's what happens.'

'You know how the Randalls and the Cowies feel about each other?'

'I know.'

Frank nodded. 'Judge Daniels is in Prudence today, so with luck, he should get here tomorrow.'

'Good.' Gabe paced to the window. He stared at the almost deserted road. 'Means we just have to worry about tonight.'

Frank turned and, with his arms folded, stared at Gabe.

'Did anyone see you arrive?'

'Not that I know of, but I've a feeling that word will get out that Max is back.'

'Max ain't popular here, but we ain't had a lynching in Carmon since I was a child. The townsfolk wouldn't have the courage for that sort of thing these days.'

'Ain't the townsfolk I'm worried about.'

'What do you mean?'

Gabe scratched his head, then planted a firm hand on Frank's shoulder.

'We'll talk later. When I return I'll help keep watch through the night, but things should be quiet for a while.'

'Where are you going?'

Gabe unlocked and opened the door.

'I'm seeing Pa. Got some questions to ask him.'

'Pa's been in a right odd mood even for Pa. You won't get any answers.'

Gabe strode into the doorway. 'Perhaps, but I ain't staying long after Daniels has been. This is my only chance to ask, while he still has a choice.'

Frank gulped. 'What choice?'

Gabe stared at the sky, noting the crisp star-filled sky. The temperature had plummeted, the first veils of a summer mist forming and drifting down the road.

'Max knows.' Gabe paced into the road.

12

'Where are Carl and Mort,' Roger Parsons whined while narrowing his eyes. 'It's getting dark.'

'I reckon they've camped down for the night,' Thomas Simmons said, his teeth gleaming in the gathering darkness. 'And we should do the same or head back.'

Roger slapped his pommel. They'd searched for three hours. He now recognized his own markings from travelling along the same length of trail.

'If they're back in Carmon supping it up in the saloon, I ain't answerable for what I'll do to them.'

'You'll have competition. I'll . . . ' Thomas drew a hand to his brow. 'One of them is coming.'

Roger stared in the same direction as Thomas. A rider galloped along the trail towards them. In the dark the form was indistinct, but seemed larger than either Carl or Mort. Roger tensed, then relaxed as he recognized the horse's distinctive white diamond pattern on the forehead.

He sat tall in the saddle and waved a hand over his head.

'Howdy, Mort. Where you been?'

'That ain't Mort. He's too big.'

As Thomas unsheathed his rifle, Roger unsheathed his too and laid it across his saddle.

The rider drew closer and slowed to a halt. He kept an arm held across his chest, the other gripping the reins low.

'I'm guessing you work for Tor McFadden,' the rider said, 'and you're looking for Mort and Carl.'

Roger glanced at the horse. Unless there were two identical horses, this was Mort's horse. He slipped the rifle deeper into his hand.

'We are. Seen them at all?'

'Saw bits of them.'

Roger glanced at Thomas. 'Bits?'

The rider winced. 'Got me a broken

arm and more scrapes beside. If you're heading back to Carmon, mind if I ride with you and I'll tell you what I know?'

Roger relaxed his grip on his rifle. 'That'll be fine with us.'

'Much obliged.'

As the rider slipped his horse closer, Roger glanced at the horse's white diamond again.

'What do you know about Mort and Carl? We've been looking for them.'

'Met them a-ways back. They were searching for Marshal Devine. Said they wanted to nail his hide to a tree and slice bits off him till what was left wouldn't fill a coyote.'

Roger chuckled. 'Yeah, that's what they were doing.'

The rider grinned. 'The trouble is, they're the ones who got their hides nailed to a tree.'

Roger flinched and, as the terrible truth hit him, the rider dropped his reins. Roger hoisted his rifle as an explosion of gunfire spewed from the rider's gun. With pain ripping across his chest, Roger tumbled from his horse, landing heavily. Through pained eyes he glanced at Thomas who lay on the ground, doubled over, the rider looming over him.

The rider fired down at Thomas's prone body, then turned to Roger.

'Devine,' Roger muttered, his breath coming in gasps.

'Got it in one.' The rider raised his gun.

*　*　*

When Gabe reached the ranch, the mist had closed in, converting the ranch house to a spectral outline. For the last time — to his current way of thinking — Gabe strode up the ranch house steps. This time, he entered without waiting for a maid.

He threw open each door in the hall until he found Roy sitting in a room by the window, staring outside.

Gabe stood in the doorway but Roy didn't move. With a snort, he strode across the room and stood over him.

With deliberate slowness, Roy turned.

'Gabe,' he said. 'Guessing you've dealt with Max.'

Gabe folded his arms. 'Yup. Except he's alive in Frank's cells.'

'Good.'

For long moments they stared at each other. Then Gabe leaned forward.

'So what is the truth about Max?'

Roy turned from Gabe's accusing eyes to stare through the window.

'You're more direct than Frank. What did Max say?'

Gabe looked through the window too, seeing only his reflection standing in the ornate room. He paced round and sat on the windowsill.

'Max reckons that you and Tor are . . . He said plenty of things, but I reckon there's something he won't tell me — some reason you want him dead.' Gabe lowered his voice to a whisper. 'Tell me what that reason is.'

'For the last few days you've been with Devine. You should know how the truth emerges.'

Gabe snorted. 'I learnt nothing from him.'

'Not his fault that you didn't learn. If you want to be a lawman, watch him.'

'I don't want to be a lawman,' Gabe snapped, his anger rising out of proportion to Roy's level comments.

'Your loss, but you're being sensible. You could never be as good as Devine is.'

Gabe gulped and turned, letting the hot flush that filled him recede. When he turned back, he shrugged.

'You don't know, do you? I thought you knew about everything before anyone else did.'

'Know what?'

'Devine is dead.'

'How?' Roy snapped, his eyes alive for the first time.

'It's a long story, but he drowned.'

'You bring the body back?'

'We didn't find one, but he'll wash up down river, probably in Monotony.'

214

Roy chuckled. The laugh grew into guffawing.

'Devine never changes,' he said between laughs. 'He used to do that when we rode together, and it always worked.'

'Do what?'

Roy mimed sleeping by cocking his head to one side and laying his hands beneath his head.

'Playing dead.'

'He ain't playing. He was mighty injured.'

Roy lifted his hands, his face as unlined as Gabe had ever seen it.

'Men like Devine need more than a few scrapes to finish them off. When he sees his situation is hopeless, he heads into the bush like a wounded animal to lick his wounds. When he's ready, and the time is right, he'll return.' Roy leaned forward and cupped a hand beside his mouth. 'Just don't tell anyone. The element of surprise is what he looks for.'

Gabe considered the fight with Devine and shook his head.

'I reckon you're wrong. But why did you call for him? Max didn't test his talents. Either you or Frank could have brought Max in.'

'We couldn't.'

'I know. Devine shoots first and doesn't care about the questions and answers. When you asked for him, you ensured that Max would die.'

'Except he's alive.'

'Plans sometimes fail.'

Silently they faced each other. Gabe heard the clock ticking. This time he was content to force Roy to talk with his silence.

'I have no plan,' Roy whispered. 'I called for Devine because he imposes his own rules. He sees through the chaos and imposes order. Guess he'll do that until the truth emerges. Not everyone will live but that's what happens when Devine's around.'

'And what charges are you inventing for Max?'

Roy stood. He strode to a cabinet and reached inside to remove a decanter, which he placed on a tray beside a single glass. He stared at the glass and frowned. His hand strayed to a bell on the cabinet. Then he bent and rummaged inside the cabinet. He emerged with another glass and placed it on the tray. Without asking he poured two measures of whiskey and returned to Gabe.

Gabe took the offered glass and sipped it.

Roy gulped his whiskey and fingered the sparkling glass.

'The legalities are out of my hands — as they have been since I called for Devine. I have faith that his law will decide the issue.'

'And the issue has to do with why Tor McFadden and you are rich and why you hate the Randalls and why Billy is marrying Thelma and . . . ' Gabe shrugged. ' . . . and everything.'

Roy sipped his drink. 'And everything.'

'And even why I'm here?'

Roy stared down into his drink,

swirling it around.

'I guess your return helped to start this end. Ain't a coincidence that you're here to see it.'

'And Ma, Martha?'

Roy coughed. 'Martha ain't involved.'

Gabe gulped his drink, letting the fire burn down to his belly. He glanced at the decanter and swirled his empty glass.

'After we've sorted this I'm heading to New York. I doubt I'll return, but I have the right to know one thing. You can keep the other mysteries, I don't care about them, but I need to know something and you can't deny me.'

Roy gulped back his drink and took Gabe's glass. He strode to the cabinet and poured another two glassfuls.

'I can deny you. Knowing the truth doesn't always help.'

'The truth never hurts, only doubt hurts.'

Roy strode back to the window. 'Spending time with Devine has helped you. Some of him has rubbed off on you.'

'It ain't,' Gabe snapped.

Roy held out his hand and Gabe took his glass. Roy licked his lips and lifted the glass, then lowered it without drinking.

'Tell me what you reckon the truth is and I'll tell you if it's true.'

Gabe took a deep breath. He'd rehearsed his thoughts but given the chance, he needed to force them from his lips.

'You had an affair with Seth Randall's wife,' he said, his voice strengthening as he forced out the worst. 'So Ma left you. Max is your son — and my half-brother — and when Max learned the truth, he took one look at everything we had and everything he didn't have and mouthed off. You called for Devine to silence him before he proved he had a claim on you.'

'Good story. How did you put that together?'

With the words said, Gabe slumped over his drink.

'I watch people. I listen to what they say and what they don't say.'

'You're trying to be like Devine, but you ain't close. He watches people. He evaluates them. He tests them. He discovers the truth. You didn't.'

'I'm sure I didn't get it all but most of it is true.'

Roy nestled his drink in his cupped hand and swirled the glass.

'You found one truth. Max was mouthing off. The rest ain't true.' Roy strode round to stare at Gabe. 'Martha was a fine woman. Seth Randall's wife wasn't. Ain't a man alive who'd have taken off with her. I hate Max, but that ain't because he has a hold on me.'

'Tell me one thing then — why did you send ma to California? Did *she* have an affair with Seth Randall?'

Roy shook his head, his eyes watering. 'You don't want the answer.'

'Don't tell me what I want.' Gabe gripped his glass tighter, his knuckles cracking. 'I just want the truth.'

The door creaked open and they

glanced up. Thelma slipped through the doorway, a night-gown wrapped around her shoulders, her feet bare.

'I heard voices,' she said. 'Hi, Gabe.'

'Hi, Thelma.'

'Thelma,' Roy muttered, 'Don't go around half-clad, it ain't — '

'I wanted to see if it was Gabe.'

'It is. Now go to bed.'

With one hand on the door, Thelma clutched her robe across her stomach.

'I wanted to ask . . . '

Roy raised his eyebrows. 'Yes?'

'I . . . '

'They got Max back, if that's what's interesting you. He's rotting in Frank's cells, as he should.'

Thelma opened her mouth, then closed it.

'Pa, Gabe.' She nodded to each in turn and closed the door after her.

When Thelma's footfalls had receded, Roy turned to Gabe.

'What do you think of your sister?' Roy said, his voice gruff. 'Your sister by blood.'

Gabe glanced down at his glass. He took another sip, seeking a feeling, but finding only numbness.

'She's a fine woman. But what's the shame you won't tell me about?'

Roy drew himself to his full height. 'Stop there. I've answered your questions. Everything else should wait until tomorrow.'

'No, Pa. Tell me.'

Roy shrugged. 'Tried to stop you, but you want the answer and so I'll give it to you. I'm your pa, but Martha — may her soul rest in peace — she ain't your ma.'

Gabe slumped. 'Can't be.'

'Is. She was your ma in every way. She raised you well, but she looked after another woman's baby.'

'Whose?' Gabe searched Roy's cold eyes.

'Name doesn't matter. She's long dead and nobody would remember her.'

'Tell me,' Gabe snapped, clutching the glass hard, aware that he was close to smashing it.

'Rosie Millbank.' Roy snorted. 'She worked where the court is now. Carmon ain't had time for her kind since we ran her out of town.'

'She was a saloon girl?'

'The cheapest and roughest in town.'

'How do you know ... How can you ...'

Roy waved his hands, a slosh of whiskey slopping to the floor.

'Don't know the details but she made sure the baby was mine, then demanded money.'

'Did you pay?'

'Nope. Called her bluff and she called mine. That's why Martha left.'

'Rosie didn't want me?'

Roy laughed without mirth. 'She wanted money, and when that wasn't available she didn't want you. But Martha was a kind woman. She said how you came into the world wasn't your fault. She took you as her own.'

Gabe released his tight grip on the glass. 'Why didn't she take Thelma and Frank?'

'I wouldn't let her. Saw no reason to keep you.'

'The truth ain't so bad.'

Roy threw back the last of his drink. 'Ain't it? You're doubly unwanted. Rosie and me produced you except neither of us wanted you.'

'And *that* is the terrible secret Max will reveal tomorrow?' Gabe knocked back the rest of his drink. 'The secret you called Devine in to suppress. The secret men have died to protect and probably Max too, soon. It doesn't seem worth it to me.'

'It ain't, but people still care about what happened in those days. But that was just the start. It's the impact today that Max will reveal.'

Gabe rubbed the cool glass against his forehead. He pushed to his feet and swayed from the effect of the whiskey on his empty stomach.

'And the Randalls have something to do with it?'

Roy stared at the floor a moment. 'Seth Randall introduced me to Rosie

Millbank. Before then, I had no time for that sort of thing, and I ain't since. He destroyed my life as good as putting a gun to my head and as much as Tor McFadden has since.'

Roy took Gabe's glass from his limp hand and strode back to the cabinet.

'That sin ain't that bad. I've known worse. Men and women raising their children alone for one.'

Roy poured two full glasses and returned to Gabe.

'It is when you're founding a new way of life in a new frontier. Tomorrow, Max will do what he sees fit and Devine will impose his law. The truth will emerge. Never doubt that. I have faith.' Roy waved his arms, sloshing the whiskey about him. 'Share my faith.'

Gabe grabbed his glass from Roy's outstretched hand.

'I share nothing with you. You didn't want me and I don't want you.'

In a single gulp Roy knocked back his drink.

'Then we have that in common.'

13

Mist shrouded Carmon as Gabe trotted down the deserted main road. He dismounted outside the sheriff's office and tapped on the door.

'You're back early,' Frank said as he opened the door. 'Fancy coffee?'

Gabe nodded and walked inside, considering Frank's unasked question.

'Me and Pa talked, but there didn't seem much reason to stay afterwards.'

Frank poured a mug of coffee from the coffee-pot on the stove.

'No sign of trouble yet. I've never seen a lynching, but I'm guessing they're noisier than this.'

Gabe gulped a slug of coffee. The cloying thickness sharpened his senses which the whiskey and the cold had spiced.

He stood by the window and

watched the swirling mist, waiting for the men who had to come.

★ ★ ★

On the edge of Carmon, five men stood beneath a gnarled tree, its twisted form dark against the closing mist.

Silas Fenshaw shivered and looked up at the tree.

'I reckon the hanging tree ain't been used for ten years,' he said.

Will Sidings chuckled. 'It's probably longer but it don't matter. It's strong enough to hold Max's worthless hide. The wood ain't rotted that much.'

'Where is Tor? He should be here.'

'Guess he's getting himself some courage.'

'Better not get too much. Won't be easy to get into the jail.'

'Any idea what his plan is?'

Silas patted the hanging tree. 'Don't know, but he'd better hurry. I wouldn't choose to spend my evenings here.'

'Yeah me too.'

A gunshot sounded and Silas swirled round, peering into the mist.

'Is that you, Tor?' he shouted.

Will fell to his knees. He collapsed face down, holding his chest.

'Raid!' Silas grabbed his gun and backed to the hanging tree. 'Fan out.'

The other three men pulled their guns and edged back, forming a circle round the hanging tree. They roved their guns back and forth as they peered into the mist, seeing only the faint outlines of trees.

A cannoning series of shots blasted, each man crying out and folding.

Silas fired, but he didn't know what he aimed at. Then hot fire blasted into his guts. He staggered back and fell.

'Will, Jed, anyone,' he shouted.

A faint whistling of the breeze around the hanging tree was the only response.

Silas threw out a clawing hand and dragged himself to Will, but when he reached him, his dead eyes stared back. Silas rolled on to his side.

'Is anybody alive?' he whispered.

Cold clamminess filled him. He stared at the mist and at the shape of a tree that appeared to move. Then he realized that a man stood before the tree and was sauntering towards him.

As the numbness crept over Silas, the man slipped through the dregs of ground mist, his vast form sharpening with every slow stride. The man had his gun pointed down, his stiff left arm held over his chest.

The man stood before the hanging tree. The swirling whiteness filled in behind him. Tendrils of mist wreathed his legs in a faint embrace. He glanced at the fallen men and as his gaze turned to Silas he smiled, with just his mouth.

'You still alive?' he muttered through clenched teeth. 'I have one bullet left. That'd be yours.'

Silas gulped as the man turned the gun on him.

★ ★ ★

Gabe yawned, stretched, and shook himself awake. He realized that he'd slept. He dashed to the window.

Outside the mist had dissolved and bright sunshine blasted down on the deserted road.

Gabe turned and scratched his chest, suppressing a last yawn.

With his hat pulled over his face, Frank sat in his chair. Snores drifted from under the hat.

Gabe stoked the stove into life and put the coffee-pot back on the top.

'What's happening?' Frank muttered with a yawn.

'Pretty much the same as when you went to sleep.'

Frank stretched. 'Good. We make a fine team. I reckon we did well, being as how that was our first time fighting off a lynch mob.'

For the next two hours, they sat in companionable silence, until the first horse trotted down the road. Deputy Wiles dismounted and wandered into the office.

'You look concerned,' Frank said. 'What's wrong?'

'I've been talking with Tor McFadden. He can't find most of his men.'

'Can't find,' Frank spluttered. 'What's that supposed to mean?'

'He said they were out working for him, but they ain't reported back.'

'With all the mist last night, perhaps they've holed up until it cleared.'

'Said as much to Tor. He didn't think it likely.'

'Then help Tor search and tell me when his men turn up.'

When Deputy Wiles had left, Frank locked the door.

'You're quiet, Gabe. You know anything about Tor's men going missing?'

Gabe shook his head and returned to staring through the window.

As the morning wore on, the level of bustle increased outside the court. The townsfolk stood in small groups and talked animatedly.

'How do they know Daniels is

coming?' Gabe asked, staring around the shutters at them.

'Like you said, word gets round.'

Gabe stiffened. Tor and Billy McFadden rode down the road. They dismounted and stood on the court steps. More men arrived and flanked them with their arms folded. The crowd backed, leaving clear space before the court.

'McFadden's men have arrived.'

Frank peered through the window. 'They have plenty more than that.'

'Should we move them?'

'Nope. They ain't doing anything and they're law-abiding men.'

Gabe stared at Tor McFadden, looking for proof that he wasn't law-abiding.

The morning wore on. Instead of the crowd getting bored and wandering away, it grew. The cafe owner erected a stall and even the saloon owner pulled a trestle-table outside and sold his wares.

As the informal mêlée peaked, a cart pulled up outside the court. A short, white-haired man alighted and strode straight into the court.

'Judge Daniels,' Frank said. 'So now we sort this out.'

* * *

When Gabe and Frank entered the court Judge Daniels was shaking Roy Cowie's hand. Ten yards back, Tor and Billy McFadden stood beside five other men who had the arrogant stances of hired guns. These were the only people in court.

Gabe strode straight to Roy, who introduced him to Daniels.

'When are we doing this?' Gabe asked.

'Ain't got all day,' Daniels said. 'Sooner we start the sooner I can head to Beaver Ridge.'

Gabe glanced at the nearly empty court. 'Shouldn't we wait until everyone arrives?'

Daniels shrugged. 'This looks like all we're getting. Most days I'm lucky to face this many, and I ain't got time to wait for anyone else to roll up.'

Gabe strode to the court's back door and opened it. In the entrance hall two burly men flanked the open court door with arms folded. The crowd stood in a semicircle in the road and watched them.

The nearest man produced a harsh smile.

'You leaving?' he asked.

'Nope. Just wondered why nobody is . . .'

Two more men outside the door wheeled round to face him.

Back inside the court Daniels was shouting out his preliminaries, so Gabe backed into the court.

Rows of raised stalls spread from either side of the central aisle. Roy Cowie and Frank had sat on one side and Tor McFadden, Billy and their hired guns had sat on the first row of the other side.

Gabe sat by Roy and turned to the front.

Daniels climbed behind his bench and banged his gavel.

'I, Judge Daniels, presiding. This court is in session and when in tarnation is someone telling me why I'm here.'

'I'll bring out Max Randall and we'll find out,' Frank said.

Daniels threw up his hands and stared at his bench.

'I've come all the way from Prudence for this. You have no warrants, no forms, nothing. Don't even know if there's a crime yet.'

Frank drew himself to his full height. 'Let me bring out Max and we'll ascertain that.'

Daniels waved his gavel at Frank. 'All right, Sheriff Cowie. Trusted you this far, I'll trust you the rest of the way.'

Frank fetched Max from the cells. When Max emerged into the court, he glared about the room, his gaze lingering on Billy McFadden.

Billy stiffened. Tor fingered his gunbelt.

Max shuffled behind the accused's podium at the front of the court.

'I'm Max Randall,' he said.

'You know that you ain't under arrest so you don't need to say anything?' Daniels said.

'I do, but I want to report something.'

'Something that needed me to come to Carmon to hear?'

'Yup. What I have to tell you will call for your talents.'

Tor McFadden rolled to his feet and swaggered to Daniels' bench.

'Before Max speaks, could I have a private word with him?'

'No,' Daniels shouted, pointing his gavel as some men would aim their guns. 'I ain't got time for more distractions. What Max has to say, I want to hear.'

'Good,' Max said with a cough. 'I can make my accusations, can I?'

Daniels shook his head. 'As I said, I've come a long way. I don't want to hear unfounded accusations. You'd better have proof of whatever it is you have to say.'

'I have, Judge Daniels.'

'You ain't,' Tor shouted. 'You know squat.'

Despite the situation, Gabe bit his bottom lip, suppressing a smile.

Max leaned on his podium. 'You know what proof I have.'

'That proof might not be too healthy for some.'

Daniels slammed his gavel three times. 'I ain't standing for any man uttering threats in my court.'

Tor lowered his gaze. He strode back to Billy and whispered something. Billy nodded. Tor sat and glared at Max, his left hand gripping his upper arm and his right hand dangling beside his holster.

'No more interruptions,' Daniels said. 'I'd like to hear what Max has to say and I'd like to see the proof.'

Max's eyes glazed for a moment. 'The proof will have to wait a while, but I'll tell you what I know.'

'Enough,' Billy shouted. 'Max, Pa made you an offer to get out of town and I'm prepared to double that offer.'

'I had two reasons for refusing that offer. First, I wouldn't live to enjoy the money. You know the second reason.'

Tor leapt to his feet. 'We ain't standing for that.'

Tor pulled his gun and in a sudden lunge, Billy swung his arm to the right, knocking the gun aside as Tor fired, but lead still clipped Max's shoulder.

With blood dribbling through his fingers, Max clutched his shoulder and toppled. Then McFadden's men pulled their guns and blasted at him.

The podium was peppered with gunshots as Daniels dived for cover.

Gabe pulled his own gun, showering McFadden's men with a burst of gunfire. With his bullets fired, he vaulted behind the first row of stalls and lay on his back, reloading.

As the gunfire echoes receded, the room returned to quiet. Gabe slipped along the stalls to Frank and Roy who had also taken cover.

'You all right, Pa?' Gabe asked.

'Never been better, boy,' Roy muttered, his eyes alive. He reached down to his holster and pulled his shining Colt. He flexed his fingers. 'It's been a while.'

The door creaked open. Roy jumped up and put a bullet in it. The door slammed shut.

Another gunshot sounded, followed by Max rolling into the stall. He clutched his shoulder and shuffled to Gabe.

'You all right?' Gabe asked, passing him a spare gun.

'Podium's shot to hell but Tor only nicked my shoulder. Did you see how many we're facing?'

'I got two, maybe three. That leaves Tor, Billy and two others in here and at least four outside against . . .'

'Three Cowies and a Randall,' Max muttered.

Roy chuckled. 'At least we have someone to use as cover.'

'Roy,' Tor shouted from the opposite stalls. 'Ain't sure what's just happened. Would like to hear from you.'

'This is just like the old days,' Roy shouted.

'It is, but the way I see it, we're on this side and you're on that side. It ain't been that way for years. We have no quarrel with each other. What's left of the Randalls is a different matter.'

'I called in Devine to resolve the Randall situation. Looks like his job was nearly over before you fired.'

'I was protecting our interests. There's no reason to carry this on.'

With his gun drawn, Gabe nudged his head above the stall.

Aside from three bodies draped over the front stall, the other men were below their stall.

'Max is here to tell the truth,' Gabe shouted. 'The truth can't hurt anyone who has nothing to hide. If that doesn't include you, I understand your need to remove him.'

'We're together in this,' Tor said.

'Then let us stand together.' Gabe stood. 'I'm standing.'

Billy bobbed his head above the stall, then stood.

'Pa,' Billy said. 'No reason to stay down.'

With a nervous glance over the stalls, Tor and the others stood.

'Come on out then, Max,' Tor said. 'And tell us what you have to say — if you dare.'

With a last glance at Gabe, Max stood and edged to the bullet-ridden podium, his gun held down.

Daniels rose from behind his bench. He rummaged on his bench and grabbed his gavel. He banged it, the sound echoing through the court.

'This court is no longer in session,' he shouted. 'We need to sort this when tempers ain't so hot and less guns are about.'

'No,' Gabe shouted. 'Max has something to say about how Tor and Roy run Carmon.'

Tor snorted and, as Gabe glared at

him, several men shouted outside. Something thudded. Somebody else cried out, followed by two more thuds and a gunshot.

All eyes turned to the door, which slammed back, rattling as it almost blasted off its hinges. Four men lay sprawled in the hall.

In the doorway, Devine stood with his feet set wide and his Peacemaker dangling from his right hand. Dust and dried blood coated him from head to foot. Filth streaked his beard. An ugly bruise on his forehead gleamed through the dirt. Lengths of wood strapped his left arm, which he held across his chest.

'Marshal,' Daniels said, 'you're looking well.'

'Judge Ronald S Daniels,' Jake roared, rolling each word. 'Sorry I'm late for your court. Permission to enter.'

'Permission granted.'

Jake swaggered into the court, nothing in his gait suggesting he wouldn't have entered if Daniels had denied him permission.

'Glad to see that Max is under arrest. It's the only thing keeping him alive. Can't say the same about two other men.'

'Devine,' Daniels shouted, pounding his gavel on the bench. 'You'll holster your weapon in my court.'

Jake slipped his Peacemaker into his belt and backed two paces.

'Done that. Get on with proceedings.'

'Ain't no proceedings going on. I'm adjourning until tempers have cooled.'

'That mean I'm free to do business?'

Daniels had only nodded a fraction when Jake had his gun pulled and aimed at Tor.

The two men behind Tor twitched their arms and two gunshots rang out, the men spinning away to sprawl over the stalls.

'Tor McFadden,' Jake roared, 'you is under arrest.'

Tor snorted. 'What's the charge?'

'Attempted murder of a lawman. That lawman would be me.'

'I ain't seen you before.'

'Your men have seen me. They told me plenty.'

Tor held his arms wide. 'Bring them in and let them tell all.'

'That ain't happening. The bits that are left ain't up to talking. But I have a better witness.' Jake chuckled. 'And that'd be Max Randall. He'll tell you everything.'

'Max ain't reliable. Everyone knows I wouldn't want to kill a lawman.'

'Except to stop him bringing in Max.'

'He knows squat.'

'Max knows how you've wormed your way into Carmon.'

'More of Max's lies.'

Jake shook his head, flakes of dried blood showering to the floor.

'He knows enough. He has a powerful desire to live and I ask myself why. I shot his kin yet he bided his time before jumping me. Scum like him ain't got the patience unless they got a greater aim in life. So I reckon we should hear what that is.'

They stood in silence. Then with a

great roar, Tor pulled his gun, the weapon training in an arc towards Max.

Jake twitched his arm and a gunshot blasted into Tor's chest.

With his gun half-raised, Tor collapsed against Billy and slid to the floor.

Jake turned to Max. 'Let's hear it. He can't stop you now.'

'Just in case anyone else tries to stop me speaking,' Max said. Moving with deliberate slowness, he lifted his gun. He glanced at Roy. 'Tor McFadden had a hold on Roy Cowie.'

Roy gulped and took several long breaths.

'Go on,' Jake shouted.

'More recent problems . . . ' Max coughed and glanced at Gabe, who nodded. 'Those problems were — '

'Don't,' Roy said, lifting a hand.

In a reflex action, Max swung his gun a few inches towards Roy.

Billy twitched his hand and a gunshot rang out.

Max collapsed over his podium, waves of redness flooding from his chest. He twitched and rolled on to the floor.

'You had no right to do that,' Jake roared, aiming his gun at Billy.

With a lunge, Billy threw his gun to the floor and hurled his hands above his head.

Jake gritted his teeth and lowered his gun.

Gabe dashed to Max's side. He knelt and laid a hand on his chest, but he couldn't stem the blood flow.

'Looking bad, Max,' he whispered.

'Guessed as much.' Max coughed, his bubbling phlegm tinged red. 'But you turned out all right.'

'Yeah?'

'Your ma raised you on her own and . . . ' Max slumped, his eyes closing.

Gabe swirled round.

Billy still had his hands raised. He jutted his chin.

'I had the right to defend my future

father-in-law,' he said.

'Max wasn't going to fire,' Gabe
shouted.

'You never know with the Randalls.'

14

With nothing to preside over, Daniels left for Beaver Ridge and everyone else wandered outside. The townsfolk in the road drifted away.

Still feeling numb, Gabe stood on the court steps as Jake sauntered outside to lean against the court door.

The remainder of McFadden's hired guns nursed their bruised heads, but Billy kicked some life into them. The men gathered his pa's body and the other bodies, and trundled them out of town in the back of a cart.

'You happy with that result?' Gabe asked, joining Roy.

Roy watched the cart leave, smiling beneath his trim moustache.

'Nope,' he said. 'Had great hopes Frank would grab hold of the situation, but he's too soft.'

'I didn't mean that.'

'I know.'

'Thought you had faith the truth would emerge.'

'It did.'

'We heard nothing. Max accused Tor of having a hold on you, but he had no proof and so that's it. The truth remains buried.'

'And what is that truth?'

Gabe rubbed his forehead. 'Tor blackmailed you about your indiscretion with Rosie Millbank, but after twenty years that relationship became more complex and you both gained, except I don't know how.'

'It's simple. Trade passes through. Tor set up arrangements with — '

'I don't care,' Gabe shouted, then lowered his voice. 'Seth Randall and Tor McFadden are dead, and you had nothing to do with either death. Nobody can touch you. You walk away with everyone you hated dead and your lies still a secret.'

'You don't understand, boy.'

'I *do* understand. You didn't call in

Devine to kill Max. You called in Devine to protect him. Tor didn't know for sure that Max knew nothing and so you wanted Devine to keep Max alive just long enough to rile Tor up and get himself killed. Now everyone who's crossed you is dead and all in the name of the law. But that's no law I recognize.'

Roy snorted. 'You saying that you'll expose me?'

'Do Frank and Thelma know about your sordid life?'

'Nope.'

'Then I won't talk.' Gabe stared down the road. A new horse approached, Thelma riding tall. Gabe shuffled closer to Roy. 'But what about Thelma? She's marrying Billy McFadden.'

Roy stared down at his hands, his eyes watering.

'Yeah. No solution is ever perfect. But he ain't like Tor. With him gone, he'll do the right thing — the corruption will end.'

Gabe narrowed his eyes. 'Thelma's part of your dealings, ain't she? You were so entwined with Tor that you sold your own daughter to keep the Cowie name unsullied.'

Roy gripped Gabe's arm as Thelma jumped from her horse.

'I had faith the right truth would emerge. I still have. Just don't — '

'I won't tell her.' Gabe turned to his sister. 'Thelma, why are you here?'

Thelma smiled. 'Heard something was happening. Thought I'd come and see what it is.'

'Return, Thelma,' Roy snapped. 'This ain't for your eyes.'

Frank and Billy wandered from the court. Billy hung his head. Frank strode to Thelma and held out a hand to help her back on to her horse.

'You need to thank Billy,' Frank said. 'He'll make a fine husband.'

'Oh?' Thelma said, turning as Billy shuffled from the court steps.

'He saved Pa's life. Max tried to kill him, but Billy saved him.'

'Billy shot ... ' Thelma's voice caught with a whimper.

'Yeah. Billy killed Max.'

Thelma hung her head a moment. With her movements slow, she turned and walked to Billy.

'Seems that I have to thank you.'

'It was nothing,' Billy whispered.

Thelma held out her hand. 'Can I see the gun you used?'

'Sure.' Billy held out his gun.

As she took the gun, Thelma frowned. On the flat of her palm, she hefted the weapon. Then with a swirl of her hand, she slipped her fingers behind the trigger and shot Billy in the chest from two feet away.

Billy staggered back and fell.

She stood over him a moment, sneered, then threw the gun on to his twitching body.

From the top of the court steps, Jake chuckled.

'Why?' Frank shouted. He dashed to Billy's side, but Billy lay still.

'Pa knows.' She glanced at Roy.

'You've always believed in the right to use force. You can kill a man if you have good reason. So did I have a good reason to kill the man who shot Max Randall?'

Roy staggered back a pace, his eyes downcast, his shoulders slumped.

'I can't say,' he whispered.

Thelma headed for the sheriff's office. She stopped on the boardwalk and laid a hand over her belly.

'When you decide if I have good reason, I'll be leaving. California might be worth a visit. I hear it's a good place to raise a family.'

* * *

In late afternoon, Gabe left the sheriff's office. He loaded his horse with a saddle-bag of provisions and a change of clothes.

Jake peeled from the court and sauntered to him.

'Ex-Deputy Gabe Cowie, if you're heading east, you can ride along with me as far as Beaver Ridge. Wrong types are out on the trail. You ain't a lawman any longer, and they might waylay a lone traveller.'

'Nope. I can take care of myself.' Gabe sighed. 'You ain't asked, but as I have no proof, I ain't said anything about Uncas, Seth Randall, or the rest. But your methods are — '

'I don't care about the opinion of some lawyer man.'

Jake spat on the ground and levered himself one-handed on to his horse and headed out of Carmon. Gabe watched him until he reached the end of the road, then turned.

Frank was wandering from his office.

'So you are leaving,' he said.

'Yeah. I'm heading to New York.'

'The coach ain't for three days.'

'I know. But I hoped I might borrow one of your fine horses.'

Frank frowned. Then a smile broke the frown. 'If you borrow one of our horses, that means you'll have to return it sometime.'

'It does.'

'Any messages for Pa?'

'Nope. But tell Thelma . . . ' Gabe slipped on to his horse and tipped his hat. 'Tell her I turned out all right.'

With his eyebrows raised, Frank nodded. 'When you put away the bad men in New York, make sure they know a Cowie did it.'

'I ain't that type of . . . ' Gabe laughed. 'I'll do that.'

Gabe swung his horse away and headed east, his long shadow before him.

15

Jake Devine dismounted a hundred yards back from the camp-fire glow.

He tethered his horse to a tree and slipped through the night. As his broken arm, strapped across his chest, was throbbing, he crept with less stealth than normal.

Closer to, he confirmed that his quarry was alone. He'd tracked Gabe for two days, but travellers often made short, late-night alliances. On the edge of the firelight, Jake straightened and rested his right hand on his hip.

Gabe poked at his fire with a stick, oblivious to Jake.

Jake snorted and sauntered round in a circle into the Gabe's line of sight.

Gabe flinched, then threw his stick into the fire and stood.

'You can join me, Marshal,' he said. 'I ain't as good at hunting as you but I bagged a rabbit earlier.'

Jake paced to the fire. 'Didn't reckon you'd want me as company.'

Gabe adjusted the skewer and turned the rabbit over.

'Been doing some thinking. I still don't agree with your methods, but I reckon I understand you now. To you the result is all that matters. How you get there's irrelevant.'

'Nope,' Jake snarled. 'You've learnt nothing about me. You're a lawman no more. Then everything changes.'

'What's that mean?'

Jake raised his eyebrows. 'It means an ex-lawman who tried to kill me shouldn't have his hands nowhere near his holster.'

With a sudden lunge, Gabe scrambled for his gun, but as his hands closed on the stock, Jake pulled his Peacemaker and fired in an instant.

Gabe staggered back to land on his side. He rolled to his knees, clutching his belly.

Jake paced forward, his Peacemaker

held down, and loomed over him.

'Why?' Gabe muttered. 'I'm no threat to you. I ain't coming back this way. Max is the only one who knew what happened and he's dead.'

'It's Devine's law.' Jake blasted his gun twice more. 'Nobody threatens me and lives.'

Jake spat on Gabe's face. Then he prised Gabe's gun into his dead fingers. He glanced at the spitted rabbit roasting over the fire. With a sneer, he kicked it away, then ground out the fire.

He searched through Gabe's belongings, finding a few dollars but not much else. He pocketed the money and scattered the remaining belongings around the camp.

As an afterthought, he slipped the rigging from Gabe's horse and left it to make its own way. Then he sauntered back to his horse.

Jake rode from the camp, heading east. As the darkness enveloped him, he whistled.